Winning her Hand

(#7 A Forbidden Love Novella Series)

Also By Bree

Historical Romance:

<u>Love's Second Chance Series</u>
#1 Forgotten & Remembered - The Duke's Late Wife
#2 Cursed & Cherished - The Duke's Wilful Wife
#3 Despised & Desired - The Marquess' Passionate Wife
#4 Abandoned & Protected - The Marquis' Tenacious Wife
#5 Ruined & Redeemed - The Earl's Fallen Wife
#6 Betrayed & Blessed - The Viscount's Shrewd Wife
#7 Deceived & Honoured – The Baron's Vexing Wife
#8 Sacrificed & Reclaimed – The Soldier's Daring Widow
#9 Condemned & Admired – The Earl's Cunning Wife (August 14, 2018)

<u>A Forbidden Love Novella Series</u>
#1 The Wrong Brother
#2 A Brilliant Rose
#3 The Forgotten Wife
#4 An Unwelcome Proposal
#5 Rules to Be Broken
#6 Hearts to Be Mended
#7 Winning her Hand
#8 Conquering her Heart (July 31, 2018)

Suspenseful Contemporary Romance:

<u>Where There's Love Series</u>
#1 Remember Me

Middle Grade Adventure:

<u>Airborne Trilogy</u>
#1 Fireflies (Now perma-free in ebook format!)
#2 Butterflies
#3 Dragonflies

Paranormal Fantasy:

<u>Crescent Rock Series</u>
#1 How to Live and Die in Crescent Rock

Winning her Hand

(#7 A Forbidden Love Novella Series)

by Bree Wolf

Winning her Hand

A Regency Romance

By

Bree Wolf

This is a work of fiction. Names, characters, businesses, places, brands, media, events and incidents are either the products of the author's imagination or used in a fictitious manner.

Any resemblance to actual persons, living or dead, or actual events is purely coincidental.

Cover Art by Victoria Cooper

Copyright © 2018 Sabrina Wolf

www.breewolf.com

ISBN-13: 978-1981061877

All Rights Reserved

This book or any portion thereof may not be reproduced or used in any manner whatsoever without the express written permission of the author except for the use of brief quotations in a book review.

To Our Families

On occasion they drive us crazy
but who would we be without them?

ACKNOWLEDGEMENTS

A great big thank-you to all those who inspire me daily, those who tell me to keep writing, those who laugh and cry with my characters and me. I love being a writer, and I could never sit down every day to do what I love without all of you. Thank you.

Winning her Hand

PROLOGUE

Stanhope Grove 1819 (or a variation thereof)

Winifred sighed as her eyes beheld the newly-wed couple across the room.

"They look happy, do they not?" her brother Griffin, the Earl of Amberly, observed, his dark brown eyes shifting to her, a touch of confusion resting in them.

"I suppose so."

Griffin frowned. "Then why do you look so glum? Is Eleanor not your friend? Are *you* not happy to see *her* happy?"

Taking a deep breath, Winifred tried to sort through the contrasting emotions coursing through her body. "Of course, I'm happy for her," she defended herself, her voice a tad harsher than intended. "I hope you do not believe me to be someone who wishes others ill?"

"Not at all." Retreating somewhat from the joyous festivities, Griffin urged her to the side and out of earshot of the nearest guests in attendance. "However, you have to admit that your outlook on marriage is rather…what shall we call it?…bleak."

Enraged, Winifred fixed her brother with a stern look, her hands coming to rest on her sides. "How can you say that, Griffin? You know as well as I do that marriage for the right reasons is a most sensible constitution. I've always said so."

A grin came to Griffin's face. *That man had the audacity to grin at her! Oh, if he weren't her brother…!* "Sensible?" he asked, eyebrows raised in question. "I admit you're the only young woman I've ever met—or heard of, for that matter—who does not at least hope for a love match."

Winifred scoffed, "Why is it that you think women ought to hope for a love match while men can consider a sensible marriage?"

Again, a wide grin split his face. "Don't start with me, Winifred. You know as well as I do that your objections have nothing to do with the rights of women." He stood up straight, and his dark brown eyes rested on her face for a long moment. Then he sighed and leaned toward her, all humour gone from his face. "I believe you're simply afraid to have your heart broken."

Winifred's mouth fell open.

"Although I cannot see why," her brother continued. "Growing up the way we did, I always assumed you'd wish for a relationship like our parents'."

Riled from her brother's words, Winifred tried to maintain her composure. After all, a lady did not strike her brother.

An earl.

Well, at least not in public.

Inhaling another deep breath, Winifred waited for her pulse to cease its frantic pace before she met her brother's enquiring gaze. "Whether you know it or not," she began, doing her best to speak slowly, lest her words tumbled about one another as they sometimes did when she was agitated, "but our parents' union is the very reason for my outlook on marriage."

Griffin's forehead creased into a frown. "But they were happy."

"Precisely."

Shaking his head, Griffin lowered his voice as it grew more and more impatient. "You're not making any sense!"

"Our parents did not marry for love," Winifred said, unable to suppress a hint of triumph in her voice. "Theirs was an arranged match. In fact," she dropped her voice to a whisper, "a few years ago, Mother confided in me and told me that before their marriage she had been taken with another man. However, in the end she chose to marry

Father because he was the more sensible choice. An infatuation offers a few blissful moments, nothing more. A union based on deeper attributes, however, ensures a lifetime of happiness." With a satisfied smile on her face, she held her brother's eyes, pleased to have made her point.

Unfortunately, Griffin seemed far from impressed. Quite on the contrary, the corners of his mouth drew upward into that annoyingly superior grin of his and his eyes lit up with mischief. "I, too, have heard that story," he laughed. "However, dear Sister, in the version I heard, it was our dear grandfather who persuaded Mother to accept the earl's proposal instead of that of a penniless solicitor." His gaze held hers, a challenging glow in them. "I suppose the deeper attributes you're referring to are fortune and family name. Nothing else. Do you truly believe those will ensure future happiness more reliably than love and affection?"

Feeling the blood drain from her face, Winifred stared at her brother. "How do you know this?"

Griffin shrugged. "Grandfather mentioned it. He seemed rather pleased with himself."

Gritting her teeth, Winifred turned to the window, forcing her gaze to focus on the lush green gardens, currently topped off with a thin layer of ice crystals.

"I apologise for speaking so bluntly," Griffin whispered into her ear. "I never meant to upset you. However, I admit that your outlook on marriage frightens me sometimes." His hand settled on her arm, and he urged her to turn and look at him. "I love you dearly," he said, his voice thick with emotion as he looked into her eyes, "and I wish for nothing more but to see you happy." He drew in a deep breath. "And while I do not wish to undermine your own capabilities, I feel compelled to tell you that your sensible way of thinking of marriage will not accomplish that task."

Winifred swallowed, her limbs suddenly feeling heavy as lead. "But they were a good match, were they not? They were so much alike. They laughed together. Read together. Rode out together. Even if they were not deeply in love, they cared about one another, did they not?" Remembering her parents, Winifred could not believe that the life she had led had been nothing but a lie, a well-hidden secret.

"They did care about each other," Griffin said, nodding his head when she turned doubtful eyes to him. "However, their feelings developed over time. They *came* to care for one another. It was nothing more but…a fortunate coincidence. That's what I'm trying to tell you. Some people are fortunate to find love in an arranged marriage. But most do not." His hands tightened on hers. "I cannot stand the thought that you might end up in a marriage without love." A soft chuckle escaped him. "For despite your insistence to be rational and sensible always, your heart loves with such fierceness and devotion rarely found in people. It deserves its perfect match."

Emotionally exhausted, Winifred did not know what to think. She loved her brother dearly. Always had he been by her side, looking out for her, protecting her, guarding her happiness. Only three years her senior, he had often acted like a man far beyond his years. Especially since the day they had lost their parents in a carriage accident.

At the thought of their parents' loss, old pain flooded Winifred's heart and her eyes misted with tears. Oh, how much she wished to have her mother by her side! She would understand, would she not? At the very least, she would be able to explain the choices she had made in her life. Had she truly chosen to marry their father due to their grandfather's insistence? Or had she simply allowed him to believe so while choosing Father for her own reasons?

More than anything, Winifred remembered her mother's warm eyes, steady and unwavering as though nothing could surprise her, as though she had all the answers. Had she not promised Winifred to aid her when the time came to choose a husband? Had she not told her that impartial eyes might judge more reliably than those blinded by infatuation? Had she not spoken to her of the need for common ground? Shared interests? Expectations? Dispositions?

But now she was gone.

And Winifred was alone in her choice.

Still, walking in her mother's footsteps made her feel connected to the woman who had always known the right course. Somehow, it made her feel closer to her as though her mother was still watching over her, guiding her hand. In any case, Winifred felt less likely to disappoint…after all, was she not heeding her mother's advice?

1

A HARD LOOK IN THE MIRROR

The fortnight after Eleanor's wedding was a blur to Winifred her thoughts were directed inward. Her friend's marriage had dragged something out into the light of day, something that Winifred had ignored for a long time.

For too long.

"I'm two-and-twenty," she mumbled as she stood in the drawing room of Atherton House, her breath misting over the window pane for a moment before it disappeared. "I'm two-and-twenty."

After their parents' death, her brother, who had just been of age at the time, had inherited his father's title and taken over guardianship of his sister. For a few weeks, they had remained at Atherton House, trying to go on with their lives before one day Griffin had come to her with an idea.

"Let's travel the world," he had said, his eyes aglow for the first time since their parents' death. "After all, what is left for us here? Sadness? Grief? Sorrow?"

"Will they not follow us wherever we go?" Winifred had

objected, her own heart weighed down heavily by their recent loss. "Do you truly think we can outrun them?"

With determination in his eyes, Griffin had shaken his head. "I'm certain we cannot. However, we need something to balance them. Something good. Something that makes us smile and laugh. We have none of that here."

In a heartbeat, Winifred had agreed, knowing that she would have followed her brother to the end of the world if he had asked. Five years had passed since that day. Five years spent everywhere but here. Five years to come to terms with the loss of their parents.

It still hurt, but they had learnt to live again.

Only now, Winifred was two-and-twenty and still unmarried.

Soon, she would be on the shelf.

Drawing in a deep breath, Winifred remembered the garden party at Stanhope Grove Eleanor had invited them to only a few weeks before her wedding. Her brother and his new wife had been in attendance as well. Diana, the new Lady Stanhope, had a little boy from her first marriage, who had been out in the gardens every day, his explorations leading him through hedges and up trees…with his stepfather's assistance, of course, as he was barely three years old.

The memory brought a smile to Winifred's lips, and she remembered that it had been that very moment that she had realised what she wanted.

Marriage. Family. Children.

Although a part of her could see herself travelling the world with her brother forever, she could not deny that another part of her craved something more.

Finally, the time had come.

If she truly wanted to be a mother, she would have to find a husband first.

And now, her own mother was not here to guide her hand.

"There's no putting it off," Winifred mumbled to her own reflection. Then she stepped away from the window and sat down at the small escritoire, pulling out a sheet of paper. Where was she to begin?

If her mother were here, what would she advise her to do?

"I'll make a list," Winifred mumbled. After all, if she was to find a suitable match, she would need to look at herself first and try to judge her character with as much objectivity as she could. Only then could she hope to discover a man among the gentlemen of the ton you would suit her person and share her interests and expectations.

But who was she? What kind of a person?

devoted
loyal
rational
compassionate

Staring at those four attributes, Winifred sighed. Certainly, it was easy to speak well of oneself, was it not? However, everyone—including herself—possessed attributes that others detected with greater ease than one could hope for when looking at oneself, most importantly, because they were far from flattering.

obstinate

Winifred scowled at the word staring back at her from the page. Still, her brother had called her that quite a few times and he knew her well, did he not? Maybe he could help her.

Instantly, Winifred shook her head. No, he would never take this seriously. He would laugh at her, then try to convince her to give up on this endeavour and then he would call her obstinate when she refused.

Despite the rather unflattering word, Winifred felt vindicated. If she only tried, tried to be honest with herself and worked on this as diligently as she could, there was a chance she could accomplish this task on her own.

Good, she thought. What else?

hesitant

As proved by her tendency to ignore even pressing matters, Winifred reluctantly listed yet another unflattering attribute. Still, she had to admit it was fitting. She did take her time making decisions, always worrying that she was about to take a wrong turn, always wanting to be certain that the decision she was about to make was the right one.

Rubbing her temple, Winifred felt the desperate wish to step away from the task at hand. However, if she did so now, she would never finish, never find a suitable match.

What about interests? Her mind suggested, and Winifred welcomed the slight change in direction with open arms. Interests were far less painful, were they not?

Quickly, she jotted down a few things that brought joy to her life.

travelling
painting
dancing

Yes, this was indeed a much safer area. And it would most certainly be much easier to discover whether a gentleman shared any of her interests. Discovering deeper aspects about his personality, however, would prove much more difficult. Who indeed would be a perfect match for her character? Someone like her? Or rather someone who was her opposite? In all ways? Or only in some?

A mild headache began pounding on her left temple, and Winifred leaned back in her chair, stilling her hands for the moment. Unable to keep herself from feeling daunted by this task, she wished her mother were there.

"Ah, there you are."

Startled by her brother's voice, Winifred flinched, and her head throbbed painfully. Glancing over her shoulder, she met his gaze.

"Are you all right?" he asked, looking her up and down, a touch of concern in his dark eyes.

"I'm fine," Winifred lied, carefully placing a hand over the sheet of paper. If her brother were to see it, he would tease her endlessly. "What is that in your hand? An invitation?"

Griffin nodded, his watchful eyes dropping to the envelop in his hand. "It is. To the New Year's Ball at Stanhope Grove." Stepping toward her, he frowned, eyes narrowed. "Am I mistaken? Or is this a new event? I cannot recall any such festivity from before we left England."

Winifred shook her head. "You're not wrong. Eleanor mentioned something at the garden party. She said it was her mother's idea to hold such a ball. Apparently, her mother was a bit miffed that Lord Hampton's Christmas Ball was spoken of as legendary." She smiled. "You know the Dowager Lady Stanhope. She tends to feel the need to surpass everyone."

Griffin laughed. "Very true. Shall we attend?"

"I would like that." It would certainly be a good opportunity to mingle and maybe spot a gentleman or two who would suit her.

"What is this?" Griffin asked, peeking over her shoulder, a touch of incredulity mixed with the usual mockery in his voice.

Flinching, Winifred jerked around in her chair to find a slow grin spread over her brother's face. "Nothing that concerns you!" she snapped, then reached for the sheet of paper.

Griffin, however, snatched it up as quick as a flash and immediately retreated to the other side of the room, his eyes eagerly roaming the page. "What is this? If I didn't know any better, I'd say it was a list of your attributes. However, why would you–?" His eyes went wide before they rose from the paper and met hers. "Tell me this is not your *sensible* way of looking for a husband!"

Gritting her teeth at the sound of the word *sensible*–the way he said it would suggest it was an insult!–Winifred stormed toward him, trying to rip the paper from his hands. Unfortunately, her brother was a good bit taller than she and at present rather disinclined to give up his trophy. "Don't you dare laugh about me! After all, you of all people should be helping me with this."

"Me?" He stared at her dumbfounded. "Why?"

Grabbing him by the sleeve, Winifred yanked his arm down and retrieved her list. "Because you know me better than anyone else," she huffed, cradling the sheet of paper to her chest. "If you weren't so immature, I wouldn't be alone in this." Swallowing, Winifred turned away as she felt the sting of tears. Never had she realised how alone she felt now that her mother was gone.

It was terrifying.

"Why do you wish to marry?" Griffin asked, his voice free of mockery. "I mean, why now? You haven't said anything on the matter since…" He swallowed, no doubt remembering their lives before the shadow of their parents' loss had fallen over them.

"Because I'm running out of time." Dabbing at her eyes, she forced the tears back down, then turned to face her brother.

A frown drew down Griffin's brows as he searched her face. "What do you mean?"

Drawing in an impatient breath, Winifred welcomed the annoyance she often felt toward her brother with open arms. "Men can afford to marry late," she snapped as though the inequality of today's world was somehow his fault. "Women, however, are not so fortunate. I'm already two-and twenty, Griffin, and if I want to have children, there is no time to lose."

For a long time, he simply looked at her, too stunned to say a word. Had it truly never occurred to him that she would get married some day?

Then he swallowed, and she could see his usual self reemerge as a glimmer of mischief came to his eyes. "You want to get married? Fine. I'll help you find your perfect match. But this," he pointed at the list still clutched to her chest, "this is not the way to go about it."

Winifred glared at him. "Do not speak to me as though I am a child. I know very well what I want and how to achieve it."

"Do you?" He laughed. That man had the audacity to laugh! Could he not see how difficult this was for her? "And what good will such a list do?"

Winifred rolled her eyes at him. "It is the only way to ensure compatibility." Swallowing the lump in her throat, she continued, "It is the only way I can think of to achieve what I had hoped Mother and Father would do for me."

Griffin's eyes bulged. "You wanted them to find you a husband?"

Frowning at him, Winifred nodded. "Why would that surprise you? Did you not hope for the same?"

Staring at her, Griffin shook his head. "To tell you the truth, I hadn't yet thought of marriage, but I'm quite certain I do want a say in it. I cannot imagine having that decision taken out of my hands."

A part of Winifred could understand his vehement demand to be included in such a life-altering decision. It echoed within her, and a delicate feeling of warmth and longing rose in her heart. Where had it come from?

"Such a list will do you no good," her brother told her, his gaze soft and yet insistent as it held hers. "Please, Winifred, abandon this nonsense and simply follow your heart." A twinkle came to his eyes. "Is there no one you care for?"

Winifred swallowed as the budding emotion in her chest roared to life, warming her chilled hands, and conjuring an image of dark green eyes, piercing in their intensity and yet kind and gentle as they looked into hers.

"Is there?" Griffin prompted, a hint of suspicion in his dark gaze.

Swallowing, Winifred shook her head, partly to rid herself of the image and partly to shake off the sense of detachment that had come

over her. "There's not," she replied, her voice hard as she forced her thoughts back to the task at hand. "Now that Mother and Father are gone, this is my only chance to find a man suited to me." She lifted the sheet of paper, and her eyes travelled over the few simple words that summed up her being. It was a pitiful sight.

For a long moment, silence hung between them before her brother inhaled a strained breath. "Do you want *my* help?" he asked, a touch of incredulity in his voice.

Lifting her gaze to her brother's, Winifred smiled. "It is kind of you to offer, and I know you mean well. However, my marriage is not something to be taken lightly, and we both know that you are not the right person for this task."

All humour left Griffin's face at her words, and the seriousness that came to his eyes was one she had never seen in him before. "I cannot deny that your words ring true," he said, his voice even, and yet, she detected a slight quiver in it as though he felt ashamed to admit the truth. "However, you must know that I would never risk your happiness, dear Sister. As immature as I am," a soft and rather apologetic grin came to his features, "I would not dare gamble with your future." Holding her gaze, he swallowed, waiting for her answer as though he did not already know it, as though he feared what she would say.

Touched by the way he had spoken to her, the way he had revealed a softer side of himself, one that was vulnerable and even afraid, Winifred placed a gentle hand on his arm. "I know you wouldn't," she whispered, noting the sense of relief that chased away the tension on his face. "This is not a question of honour, but of ability. This is something you cannot do for me."

Frowning, he looked at her. "Why not? You must admit that there is no one else in the world who knows you as well as I do. Or do you disagree?"

"I do not, but—"

"Then let me help you. Please! Let me do for you what you'd hoped Mother and Father would."

Staring at Griffin, Winifred could not believe her ears, could not fathom the sudden change she saw in her brother. Always had he been light-hearted and impulsive, smiling his way through life, charming others as easily as drawing breath. Had she misjudged him? How could she not have seen this serious side of him? "Are you saying you want to find me a husband?"

21

A soft chuckle escaped him, and within an instant, the old Griffin was back. "*Want* may be a bit of a stretch, but yes. I will help you. You're my sister, and I will not leave you alone in this. Please allow me to do so."

Hesitating, Winifred looked at him, saw the earnest concern and devotion in his eyes and noted the touch of humour curling his lips. What was she to do? Certainly, he knew her well. There was no denying that. But given his character, could he take this seriously? Could he see this through? Or would he abandon her once he grew tired of this new game?

No, no matter what he would not abandon her. Still, was it wise to defer to him in this matter? Without hesitation, without a doubt in her mind, Winifred would have allowed her mother to find her a suitable husband, but her brother? Could he do this?

"I promise I will not disappoint you." Grasping her hands, Griffin looked into her eyes, urging her to believe him. "I understand why you would be hesitant." There was that word again! "But you have no reason not to trust me. And to prove it to you, I shall offer you a deal."

"A deal?" Winifred frowned. "What do you mean?"

Her brother took a deep breath as though needing to fortify himself. "Allow me to find you a husband," he said, "and I shall grant you the same permission when it comes to finding my wife."

WELCOME HOME

Stepping out of the carriage, Trent Henwood, Earl of Chadwick, allowed his gaze to sweep over Atherton House, an imposing country estate and the place that held his dearest childhood memories. A smile curled up his lips as he remembered the many summers of his youth spent here with Griffin and his sister Winifred.

Winifred. Her name immediately conjured an image of a young lady with rich auburn tresses that framed her kind face, matching those chocolate brown eyes of hers that had the power to upend his world…or set it right.

As he began to climb the steps toward the front door, Trent felt his heart beating in his chest, louder and faster than he had ever been aware of. Always had Winifred managed to keep him on edge with her serious demeanour, always trying to appear older and more mature, often chiding him and her brother for their wild ways. To this day, he remembered how she had stared up at him at age twelve, her hair pulled back in a serious knot, her arms crossed and her right foot tapping with annoyance at the way he and Griffin had come running into the drawing room, knocking the tea tray to the floor with a loud clatter. Oh, even then those eyes of hers had known how to shoot fire!

With a deep breath, Trent stepped over the threshold and greeted the old butler. "Good day, Harmon. How is the knee?"

"Quite all right, my lord." The old man smiled at him. "It's good to see you again."

Nodding, Trent gazed at the familiar hall with the sweeping staircase leading to the upper floor. How often had he and Griffin slid down the banister when no one was looking? How often had they been caught nonetheless?

A smile curled up his lips at the memory.

"Those were good days," the old butler remarked with a wicked gleam in his eyes that Trent remembered only too well.

"They were indeed," he agreed, then glanced toward the old study tucked away in the eastern side of the house. "Is he in?"

Harmon nodded. "His lordship is in the study…and Lady Winifred is painting in the conservatory."

About to take a step, Trent froze, his right foot lifted off the ground, slightly offsetting his balance. Then he cleared his throat and set it down, glancing at Harmon's unreadable face. "Thank you," he stammered as every fibre in his being strained toward the conservatory. "I shall…speak to his lordship first," he said nonetheless, forcing his feet down the eastern corridor.

His footsteps' echo reached his ears, flying ahead as though to announce his arrival. It was a familiar sound, and Trent could not believe that it had been five years since he had last heard it.

When his mother had died giving birth to him, Trent's father had been heart-broken, retreating from the world and his only child, only knowing grief and sorrow, wandering Tredway Manor like a ghost. Thus, the first few years of Trent's life had been marked by loneliness.

Eton had changed that.

On the very first day, he had met Griffin and a lifelong friendship had grown between them. From then on, Trent had spent every free minute at Atherton House, finding a surrogate home with Griffin's family who had welcomed him with open arms. The death of the siblings' parents had affected him as much as his own father's passing a few years past…if not more. After all, they had been the ones to counsel and comfort, chide and praise him.

When Griffin and Winifred had left England, he had been devastated, wishing he could have joined them. However, his late father's affairs had demanded his attention, and he could not in good conscience have left his estate and all those who depended on him to travel the world.

But now they had returned, and the moment he had heard the news, Trent had dropped everything and hastened over.

Home, a quiet voice whispered as he came to stand outside the study, reminding himself that he would not find the old earl on the other side, but his friend instead.

After knocking, he entered upon hearing Griffin's voice and could not help but stare—at least for a moment—at the man he had not seen in five years, the man that had been like a brother to him, the man he had missed dearly for too long.

Stepping around the desk, Griffin strode toward him, a deep smile on his face. "It's been too long, old friend," he announced as though chiding Trent for staying away. Then he pulled him into a fierce embrace. "It is good to see you, Brother."

Inhaling deeply, Trent returned Griffin's hug with the same mixture of longing, regret and joy. "How long have you been back?"

Stepping back, an apologetic grin came to Griffin's face. "A couple of weeks."

"Weeks?" Trent's eyes bulged, and a touch of disappointment washed over him.

"Winifred received an urgent message from a friend," he said by way of explaining.

"A friend?"

"Lady Eleanor," Griffin elaborated. "I mean Mrs. Waltham now."

"I remember her well," Trent said, wondering why *he* had never written, asking them to come home. "I heard that she'd married."

"Yes, a small ceremony a fortnight ago at Stanhope Grove."

Trent frowned. "Knowing the dowager countess, I would have expected a grander event, especially after Lord Stanhope's marriage to the young widow within a few weeks after her husband's passing was an equally private affair."

A wicked grin came to Griffin's face. "Sometimes love cannot wait for a large wedding. However, I have to say the dowager countess seemed quite pleased with the development although I cannot say why." He shrugged. "Something happened during our visit that we weren't all made privy to."

Griffin drew in a deep breath, and the humour left his face.

Then his gaze shifted to Trent's, and yet, he did not speak.

"Is everything all right?" Trent asked, feeling his skin crawl with apprehension. "You seem out of sorts."

With all his heart, Trent wished he had the courage to ask about Winifred. However, he did not dare reveal how he truly felt about her to his friend. Hell, it seemed he had only just realised it himself! After their departure, he had come to realise that his longing for her was different from the way he longed to see his oldest friend again. Always had they been family to him, and he knew he loved them dearly. Still, the way he thought of Winifred did not speak of brotherly affection. How would Griffin react if he found out?

"I'm not certain," Griffin finally said, the expression on his face rather tense while his eyes seemed to search Trent's face. "I've entered into a rather unfortunate pact with my sister."

"Winifred?" Trent all but croaked, revelling in the feeling of her name on his tongue. It had been too long since he had been able to say it! "What do you mean?"

Griffin inhaled a deep breath, his gaze unwavering. "She wants me to find her a husband."

Shock slammed into Trent like a charging bull, and he sucked in a sharp breath, trying to ease the pain radiating through his heart. "A husband? Is she…? I mean does she…already have a certain gentleman in mind?"

Griffin's gaze narrowed before the left corner of his mouth tugged up into a wicked grin. "May I ask you a question?"

Swallowing, Trent nodded.

"Why did you never ask for her hand?"

Trent's eyes bulged as the charging bull hit him square in the chest for the second time that day. "I beg your pardon?" he stammered, suddenly feeling light-headed.

Clasping a hand on his friend's shoulder, Griffin held his gaze. "A blind man could see that you love her, have loved her for a long time." The hint of a frown came to his features. "I understand that she was too young when we left, but to tell you the truth I have been waiting for you to come find us, find her, ever since. Why didn't you?"

Shaking his head as though that could dispel the truth of what he had just heard, Trent tried his best to swallow the lump in his throat. Indeed, why had he not? "Does…does she know?"

Griffin laughed, "Oh, even if she did, she would never admit it to herself. After all, she does not believe you to be a *sensible* choice." He shook his head in annoyance before the humour left his eyes. "However, I do believe she cares for you...if only she were brave enough to admit it."

Did she truly care for him? Could it be possible? Involuntarily, Trent's heart began to dance in his chest before he forced it back into the sad, little room where it had lived these past five years. "I do not believe what you say is true. After all, whenever we lay eyes on one another, all we do is—"

"Bicker?" Griffin cut in. "Yes, I've noticed. Maybe it's time you stop treating her like a little girl. After all, it's been five years."

Disheartened, Trent shook his head. "Quite frankly, I don't know how else to speak to her."

"You've never seemed particularly shy around the fair sex," Griffin observed with a grin. "Why now?"

Trent shrugged. "I wish I knew."

"So, you care for her?"

Trent sighed, forcing himself to meet his friend's gaze. "As you've so shrewdly observed, yes, I do." Again, he tried to swallow the lump in his throat. Again, without success. "Is there a particular gentleman courting her?"

Griffin grinned at him, amusement twinkling in his eyes. "Not at present. After all, we've only been back in England for a few weeks, and the Season has yet to start." For a moment, he looked at Trent, his gaze full of meaning. "However, I doubt that she will be lacking suitors."

Trent nodded, feeling more disheartened by the minute. How was he to go about winning Winifred's heart as well as her hand if he was to compete with the finest gentlemen London had to offer?

After all, in her presence he seemed to lack any kind of finesse. Where otherwise he would be charming and agreeable, striving to be attentive and offering compliments, he knew he was unable to do so when the woman he loved was near. As soon as her gaze fell on him, challenging and daring, he could not help but tease her. In truth, he loved the way she had always rolled her eyes at him, lit up with the fire she all too often kept firmly bottled within.

"There's another matter that complicates things," Griffin added, wringing his hands as though nervous. A rather unusual sight!

"What is it?"

"Since our parents can no longer assist her," he said, his voice grave, "I've offered to aid her in finding a suitable match. However, she was rather reluctant to allow me to help. In the end, I only gained her acceptance by offering her my trust in exchange for hers."

Trent frowned. "What do you mean?"

Griffin licked his lips, a disbelieving smile tugging on the left corner. "She agreed to let me find her a suitable match—according to her own directives, of course—if I agree to the same, meaning allow her to choose my future wife."

Trent was certain his mouth dropped open for a moment. "You did what?"

"I know. I know. It wasn't my finest moment," Griffin agreed. "However, I could not allow her to choose for herself. As I said she was going about it in her usual *sensible* manner, and believe what you want, but I'm convinced it would only make her miserable. I had to step in."

"So, she wants you to find her a husband?" Trent asked carefully. "She's leaving the choice completely to you? She will marry whomever you choose?"

Griffin frowned. "Within reason, yes, I suppose so." Then his gaze met Trent's, and a large smile curled up his lips. "I can see what you're thinking. However, I will not sacrifice my own happiness because you're afraid to declare your feelings. I know my sister; she would exact revenge in a most *sensible* way." He scoffed, then turned serious eyes on Trent. "I cannot go over her head. I need to take her demands seriously."

"I understand." Trent nodded, knowing that it would be wrong to persuade Winifred into a marriage she did not want to choose freely. Still, for a moment, he had been thoroughly tempted.

"If you want her hand in marriage," Griffin counselled, "you need to win her heart first." He sighed rather theatrically. "And preferably before I'm forced to choose one of those mind-numbingly boring gentlemen Winifred currently has her eye on for my future brother-in-law. Believe me, everyone wins if you can find a way to convince her that she's in love with you and that that is a *sensible* reason for marriage." Shaking his head, Griffin rolled his eyes. "Are we in agreement?"

Staring at his best friend, Trent grasped the offered hand and nodded. "I shall try," he mumbled, feeling his heart ache in his chest as failure and all its consequences loomed on the horizon. Had anyone ever been able to convince Winifred of something she did not want to believe?

"Don't try, my friend," Griffin warned. "Do! Failure is not an option, or all our lives will take a turn for the worst."

3

A GENTLEMAN & A LADY

Stanhope Grove sparkled with lights and laughter that New Year's Eve, and Winifred found herself bewitched by the joyous atmosphere brought on by the promise of a new year and everything it might bring. Music echoed through the vaulted ballroom as couples danced until exhaustion, their cheeks bright red and their eyes aglow, perfectly attuned to the face-splitting smiles that seemed so common that night.

"Is it not wonderful?" the dowager countess beamed, her usually stern expression lost, replaced by one of proud delight. "Is it not the most magnificent ball you've ever attended?"

Noting the way Eleanor rolled her eyes as her mother chased one compliment after the other, Winifred smiled at the dowager countess. "It is indeed. I do believe it shall soon become a legendary event greatly anticipated throughout the entire year."

Instantly, the dowager countess beamed with pleasure, and Winifred looked at her friend, noting the way she shook her head at her, a grateful smile on her kind face.

A moment later, the dowager countess hastened away, no doubt in search of more admirers.

"It was sweet of you to indulge her." Squeezing Winifred's hand, Eleanor smiled at her. "I know she can be quite tiresome in her exuberance."

Winifred chuckled, knowing her friend's words to be an understatement.

"What is so amusing?" Griffin asked as he walked toward them with Eleanor's husband, Henry Waltham, by his side.

"Nothing that would concern you," Winifred said to her brother, unwilling to discuss the dowager's need for compliments any longer than necessary. So, before he could enquire further, she turned to her friend's husband. "It is so good to see you again, Mr. Waltham. I hope marriage is treating you well."

Mr. Waltham smiled, and his gaze momentarily drifted to his wife. As their eyes met, Winifred could have sworn that the lights around them had dimmed—only for a moment as though they knew they could not compete. Then he looked back at her and nodded, gently pulling his wife's hand through the crook of his arm. "Very much so."

Still at odds about her friend's way of procuring a husband—namely falling in love—Winifred watched as Mr. Waltham led Eleanor onto the dance floor.

"They do look happy, do they not?"

Glancing at her brother, Winifred nodded. "They do right now. But how long will it last?"

"No one can know that," Griffin counselled, and she knew from the way he spoke that he was not merely making an observation but meant to prove a point. "While some arranged marriages end in love, some love matches are reduced to a marriage of convenience. These things happen. No one knows the future. We can only ever make the most out of what we do know."

Turning to look at her brother, Winifred narrowed her eyes. "And what is that?"

"How we feel." Holding her gaze, he shrugged. "What we want. What we believe makes us happy."

Getting annoyed with his lectures, Winifred crossed her arms in defiance and fixed him with an icy stare. "I know what you are trying to do, dear Brother, and I am telling you it will not work. I do know what I want as I have told you more than once. You agreed to help me if you haven't forgotten."

With his lips pressed into a thin line, Griffin nodded.

"I'm glad, for your behaviour would suggest otherwise," Winifred chided. "You've done nothing but try to dissuade me from the course I've chosen. So, let me ask you: do you wish to be released from your obligation or will you finally take it seriously?"

Defeat on his face, Griffin held her gaze for a long moment. Still, Winifred could almost see his thoughts racing, trying to think of a way to sway her after all. He was nothing if not relentless!

"Fine," he said, throwing up his hands. "I give up. You win."

Winifred scoffed, "I hardly would call that winning. Did we not agree on this in the first place?"

Grumbling under his breath, Griffin nodded once more.

"Then I would suggest you…" Her voice trailed off as she glanced around the room at the attending gentlemen. Was a suitable man here tonight?

Griffin sighed as though he had been asked to muck out the stables with nothing but a fork. "All right," he grumbled, annoyance clear in his voice. "Then tell me which gentleman strikes your fancy."

Spinning around, Winifred glared at her brother. If she did not know any better, she could swear he did this on purpose simply to aggravate her!

"All right. All right." Throwing up his hands in surrender, he stepped back. "I shall see what I can find out about the eligible bachelors present tonight." He gestured to the dance floor. "You go and enjoy yourself. I suppose someone should." As he walked away, Winifred heard him grumble under his breath, "Now, she's got me hunting down men instead of…" His voice trailed off as his attention was momentarily diverted by a fair-haired beauty in a stunning blue gown.

Winifred sighed in exhaustion. What had she been thinking? Could Griffin be trusted to find her a suitable match? Or was this endeavour doomed from the start?

Oh, how she wished her mother were there!

"Good evening, my lady."

At the sound of his voice, the air rushed from Winifred's lungs, and her heart almost jumped out of her chest. Closing her eyes for but a moment, she felt goose bumps dance up and down her skin.

Then Winifred jerked her eyes back open and, brushing her hands over her arms to chase away the chill, willed her nerves back under control. Turning around to face him, she could only hope that her emotions were not written all over her face.

"Are you cold?" Trent asked, a concerned frown drawing down his brows as his dark green eyes met hers.

Searched hers.

Held hers.

Winifred swallowed, trying to focus on the words he had spoken. "I'm fine," she finally said, her voice barely a whisper. How long had it been since she had last seen him? Had it truly been five years?

A few weeks ago, he had come to Atherton House to visit Griffin. However, he had not come to see her. Only after he had already left, had her brother informed her of Trent's visit, and her heart had ached rather painfully at being overlooked thus. Had they not all been close once? Did he not care for her as he cared for her brother?

A smile curled up Trent's lips as he formally bowed his head to her. "It is good to see you here, Lady Winifred. I hope you enjoyed the continent."

Lady Winifred? Swallowing, Winifred frowned. Never in his life had Trent spoken to her in such a civilised manner. What was he up to? "It was pleasant. Quite diverting."

"I'm glad to hear it."

Moments ticked by as they looked at each other. Would he not say more? She wondered. Would he not tease her as he always had?

When the silence became awkward, Winifred groped for something—anything—to say. "I would ask you not to sneak up on a lady," she chided, her voice harsher than she had intended. "It portrays a severe lack of manners." Shrugging, she sighed, "But then again, you never had any." The moment the words left her lips Winifred realised what she had said, and her teeth clenched in mortification. It was all she could do not to cover her mouth in shock.

Trent, however, seemed neither shocked nor offended. In fact, his sparkling green eyes seemed to light up from inside as though she had just answered his most fervent prayers. His face split into a wicked grin as he stepped forward and leaned in conspiratorially. "You know me too well, Fred."

Fred! There was that name again!

"I'd be much obliged if you would refrain from addressing me thus," she huffed, doing her best to sound outraged and ignore the little somersaults her stomach did as his breath brushed over her cheek.

"It's been five years," he whispered in her ear. "I've missed you."

Winifred swallowed before her eyes sought his. He'd missed her? Never had he... "You've missed me?" she scoffed, rolling her eyes at him. "Or rather you've missed teasing me? Is that not true? Were you unable to find another woman willing to put up with your manners?"

His smile deepened, and a wicked gleam came to his eyes. "I must admit you never seemed particularly willing, dear Fred. However, I'm glad you've cleared that up. Now, that you're back, I shall not leave your side. After all, we have a lot of time to make up for."

"I'm afraid I must disappoint you." Taking a step back, Winifred squared her shoulders and raised her chin. "At present, I find myself rather," she groped for words yet again, "occupied." Why was it that this man always made her feel like a woman without sense?

"Occupied?" He grinned, once more closing the distance between them. "Doing what?"

"That is none of your concern." She took another step back.

His eyes flashed. "Sounds intriguing. Tell me more."

"I shall not."

"Why?" Again, he took a step closer, unwilling to let her escape.

Rolling her eyes, Winifred felt the familiar feeling of utter annoyance flare to life. "Because it does not concern you!"

At the pitch in her voice, he grinned. "You've already said that."

Crossing her arms over her chest, Winifred glared at him. "Were you born this irritating?"

"What can I say?" He shrugged. "You bring out the best sides of me."

"Hardly." Unbelievable! The nerve that man had!

Unexpectedly, he offered her his arm. "May I have this dance?" he asked, glancing at the dance floor where couples stood up for a cotillion.

Taken aback, Winifred did not know what to say. A part of her almost desperately wanted to know what it would feel like to sweep across the dance floor in Trent's arms. However, at the same time, warning bells went off in her ears! There was something dangerous about him, and if she was not careful, he would upset her carefully thought-out plans.

"I'm afraid I must decline," Winifred said, and for a moment, the touch of honest disappointment that came to his eyes robbed her of all rational thought. "However, I...I've promised this dance to my

brother. Therefore, I must take my leave."

As she turned away, her heart pounding in her chest like never before, Trent suddenly stepped into her path, holding out an arm to keep her from stealing past him.

Frowning, she glared at him. "What's the meaning of this?" No manners whatsoever, it would seem!

"I apologise." Still, the look on his face was far from apologetic. In fact, he looked very pleased with himself. Smug even. "However, Griffin asked me to step in for this dance."

Winifred frowned. How could he have? After all, it had been a lie.

"He told me he was rather *occupied* with some sort of *project* you asked him to assist with," Winifred froze, "and knowing how much you love it, he did not wish for you to miss the chance to dance."

Staring at Trent, Winifred felt the blood drain from her face. Did he know? Had Griffin told him? The way he had stressed the words *occupied* and *project* suggested a deeper meaning. Was he teasing her? Did he know and now wanted nothing more but to see her squirm?

Forcing a calming breath into her lungs, Winifred swallowed, willing her muscles to relax. "If that is what he said." Then she lifted her hand and placed it on his, allowing him to lead her onto the dance floor.

The warmth of his hand—even through her glove—sent a jolt through her body, which made her draw in a sharp breath.

"Are you all right?"

Willing a noncommittal smile onto her face, Winifred nodded. "Perfectly fine."

As the music started to play, all the couples began moving up and down the line. Relieved, Winifred concentrated on the steps, the rhythm, anything but the man across from her.

"You seem flustered."

Her eyes snapped up. "I'm not!"

"As you wish," he said with a chuckle.

After that, they managed a few steps in silence. Still, she could feel his eyes on her and wondered what he was up to.

"Your brother seems to be enjoying himself."

Frowning, Winifred looked at Trent, then followed his gaze down the line…where her brother was dancing with the fair-haired beauty in the stunning blue gown, who had caught his attention before.

Heat shot up Winifred's face at having her lie pointed out to her so bluntly.

Still, she refused to submit to defeat. Instead, she turned her glower onto the man who deserved it. "I admit it was an excuse—"

"It was a lie," he corrected smiling as though he was enjoying this...which he probably was. "You lied to me."

Winifred gritted her teeth. "As did you."

A frown drew down his brows. "Care to enlighten me?"

"You said my brother had asked you to step in," she elaborated, wondering how Trent could know about their *project* if he had indeed never spoken to Griffin. "Was that not also a lie, *my lord*?"

"It most certainly was," he admitted freely, drawing her arm through his before he led her off the dance floor and toward the refreshment table.

Frowning, Winifred only now noticed that the music had stopped, and the dance ended.

"You seem parched," Trent observed, handing her a glass of lemonade, his eyes smiling as he stepped closer and his arm brushed hers. "I must say lying becomes you."

Winifred flinched, feeling mortified when he laughed.

"Your cheeks are flushed. Your eyes are glowing." Then he sighed as though he were an art enthusiast gazing at a masterpiece. "Looking like this, you are the image of…"

Unable to stop herself, Winifred prompted, "Of what?"

Instantly, that wicked gleam was back in his eyes. "I fear I must think on that."

Inside, Winifred wilted. Were they truly unable to speak to each other in a civilised manner? What did that say about them? About her? Thinking of her list of attributes, Winifred wondered if she ought to amend it. Was she a petty or even vindictive person? Why could she not let go of the past and meet Trent with a clean slate? After all, it had been five years.

Inhaling a deep breath, Winifred set down her lemonade. "Then I shall leave you to it. Good day, my lord." And without looking over her shoulder, she marched to the other side of the large room, grateful when she spied Eleanor and her husband leaving the dance floor.

"Are you all right?" her friend asked when Winifred drew near. Then she cast a meaningful glance at her husband, who promptly excused himself. "Is something wrong?"

Winifred shook her head, unable to explain the turmoil that had been her constant companion since Trent had materialised behind her. And so, she inhaled another deep breath, forced a delighted smile on her face and said with as much enthusiasm as she could muster, "Not at all. In fact, I'm enjoying myself quite profusely."

Eleanor smiled. "I'm glad to hear it." Still, there was a hint of doubt in her eyes.

Swallowing, Winifred allowed her gaze to sweep across the guests in attendance, only excluding the area around the refreshment table. "Are you well acquainted with most of your guests?" Seeing the slight frown on Eleanor's face, she added, "As I've been out of the country for so long, I fear I hardly know anyone."

Instead of dissipating, the frown on Eleanor's face grew deeper and a hint of suspicion came to her eyes. "Tell me what is going on, Winifred? You seem…not like yourself."

Winifred sighed. Oh, how right her friend was!

"Well, quite frankly, I have decided that it was time I chose a husband."

Eleanor's eyes widened. "You have?"

"Yes, I've already spoken to Griffin, and he's assured me he will do his utmost to find me a suitable match." Her eyes narrowed as she craned her neck but failed to spot her brother. "Although keeping his mind firmly fixed on this task seems to be an act of futility."

"Your brother?" Eleanor asked, her voice momentarily filled with confusion before her eyes opened wide. "You want *him* to choose your future husband?"

Winifred looked at her friend. "Of course. Since my parents are no longer with us, he is the logical choice." A frown drew down her brows at the surprise on her oldest friend's face. "I cannot understand why this would surprise you. Have we not spoken about this subject only recently?"

"We have," Eleanor conceded. "However, I…I cannot believe you would truly do this."

Again, Winifred frowned. "Why wouldn't I?"

"Because…" Shaking her head, Eleanor seemed to be groping for words. Seemingly, it was that kind of evening! "What about love? I know you're rather practical, but is there no one you care for?"

Annoyed at this repeated suggestion from the people who ought to know her best, Winifred tried to contain her anger. "You sound like my brother!" she snapped, instantly regretting the harshness in her tone.

Eleanor, however, did not seem to have noticed as her gaze drifted across the ballroom to the refreshment table. Then she looked at Winifred and taking a step closer whispered, "What about Lord Chadwick?"

Unprepared for this shock, Winifred momentarily feared she would lose her balance. "Trent?" she all but stammered, trying to keep her wits about her.

In answer to Winifred's reaction, Eleanor's eyes lit up and her lips curled up into a knowing smile. "Trent, is it?"

Winifred huffed, arms akimbo. "We grew up together. He's like a brother to me."

Eleanor scoffed, "He certainly does not look at you as a brother would." Holding Winifred's gaze, she bobbed her head up and down. "You know that as well as I do. Does he make you feel like Griffin does when he's near you?"

Winifred swallowed.

"See?"

"See what?" Remembering Trent's teasing, his obnoxious insistence on calling her Fred, Winifred had trouble holding on to her manners. "If you must know that man is the most annoying, insufferable and completely inappropriate person I've ever met. That is how he makes me feel! So, whatever you hope to accomplish by this line of questioning, I assure you it will not dissuade me. No, we do not suit one another. I wish for a husband who shares my interests, who understands my character because we are alike, because we have the same expectations in life."

"And you think Griffin will find such a man for you?"

Drawing in a deep breath, Winifred mumbled, "He better, or I swear I will make him pay."

4

WHAT TO LOOK FOR IN A HUSBAND

Watching her walk away from him, Trent cursed himself. After all, he had come to Stanhope Grove with every intention of treating her as a gentleman would treat a lady. However, old habits seemed to die particularly hard where Winifred was concerned. The moment she had snapped at him as she had so many times before, he had not been able to resist.

He had even called her *Fred* although he knew perfectly well how much she detested that name. Still, he enjoyed teasing her. The way her eyes lit up with fire, shooting arrows at him, entranced him. He could not say why or how, but on some level, he could swear she enjoyed their bickering as well.

Looking across the ballroom, he saw her speaking to Mrs. Waltham, relieved that at least at present she was not in the arms of another gentleman. The thought alone turned his stomach.

Still, he knew it was inevitable.

After all, she was a rare beauty, was she not? Even if he had not been in love with her, he would have thought her magnificent, the way her dark brown eyes shone in the candle light, the grace with which she had moved when she had followed him during their dance. She had truly grown into a remarkable woman, witty and clever, but also kind and loyal, and with a wicked sense of humour that matched his own.

In that moment as Trent stood on the far side of the ballroom, gazing at the woman he had loved from afar for five years, he finally realised how much he had missed her. How had he survived the past years without seeing her? Without speaking to her?

Glancing at her brother, Trent gritted his teeth as he saw Griffin's gaze drifting over the assembled guests, trying to pick out potential suitors, no doubt. Although his friend seemed annoyed with the task, Trent knew that there was no one in the world whom he loved more dearly than Winifred. She was the one who commanded his loyalty and devotion above everyone else, and he would not fail her.

Again, Griffin's words echoed in his ears. *If you want her hand in marriage, you need to win her heart first. Failure is not an option, or all our lives will take a turn for the worst.*

That day when he had hastened to Atherton House to see his friends after their long absence, Trent had only spoken to Griffin. Although he'd had every intention of seeing Winifred—in fact, it had been the foremost thing on his mind—Griffin's revelations had shaken him to his core and he had needed time to regain his balance, to decide on a course of action to start fresh and prove to Winifred that he could be the man she wanted.

However, so far, he'd only made a mess of things! If the looks she occasionally cast in his direction were any indication, he had managed to anger her quite thoroughly. In fact, she seemed spitting mad!

Throughout the evening, Trent continued to watch the woman he loved dance with one *suitable* gentleman after another while he cursed himself, her and her efficient brother. Did Griffin have to introduce her to all these men? Could he not at least buy Trent a little more time?

Would it matter? A rather annoying voice whispered in his head. *Either she cares for you or she does not.*

Did she?

Seeing the gentle smile on her face as she conversed eagerly with her current dance partner, Trent doubted it very much. For if she liked these *suitable* men, she could never like him, could she? Did that smile on her face truly speak of a certain partiality on her side or was

she simply displaying better manners than he had ever possessed?

With each dance, the knot in his stomach twisted and turned, and when the last notes of yet another piece drifted away, Trent strode forward without conscious thought. All he knew was that he would not stand idly by and watch other men sweep Fred off her feet.

So, when she inclined her head to her dance partner and turned to leave, he was there, right in front of her, blocking her path.

Startled, her gaze narrowed, and the soft brown of her eyes ignited instantly. "What are you doing here?" she snapped, casting careful glances around them, trying to keep her voice down despite the anger that made her shoulders tremble. "Let me pass."

Stomping on the fear that had grown in his heart throughout the night, Trent held out his hand to her, doing his best to appear the perfect gentleman. "May I have this dance?"

Instantly, suspicion came to her eyes, and his resolve faltered. How could he ever hope to win her heart if he had to pretend to be someone he was not?

"I'm afraid I've already promised the next dance to Lord Haverton," she told him, satisfaction as well as a hint of a challenge in her voice.

"Lord Haverton?" Trent mumbled as he took a step closer, his gaze fixed on her face. "And does the gentleman know that he has asked you for the next dance?"

Immediately, her lips clamped shut, and steam seemed to be coming out of her ears. "I would appreciate it, my lord, if you would refrain from calling me a liar."

Trent chuckled, "I've good reason to, in case you've forgotten." However, glancing around, he saw a good-looking gentleman heading straight toward them, his gaze fixed on Winifred. "As you wish," Trent said, turning back to her. "However, then I must insist you save me the next dance."

Grinning, she asked, "Why ever would I do that?"

Inhaling a deep breath, he stepped closer and grasped her wrist, surprised to feel her pulse hammering as she tried to tug her hand free. "Believe me, dear Fred," he whispered, and her gaze narrowed, "you would not want to cause a scene. What would all those eligible bachelors think of you?"

At his question, all colour drained from her face and she stared at him, her mouth slightly open. "How do you...? I..."

"Are we in agreement?" he prompted as Lord Haverton drew

near.

Winifred swallowed. "Fine."

Reluctantly, Trent released her wrist and nodding to Lord Haverton took his leave. However, from the side of the ballroom, he watched them dance, watched as Lord Haverton tried to make polite conversation, watched as Winifred did her best to answer courteously. Still, her gaze often travelled to him, and Trent could not deny that he felt a deep sense of satisfaction that he had managed to occupy her thoughts so thoroughly.

The moment the dance ended, Trent strode forward and instantly relieved Lord Haverton of his dance partner. Pulling her farther onto the dance floor, Trent rejoiced when the first notes of a waltz began to echo through the large room.

Meeting Winifred's gaze, he reached for her. The moment his hand settled on her waist, she drew in a slow breath. Her gaze, however, remained firmly on his. Only now, her eyes held no anger or annoyance. Now, they held something else entirely.

Encouraged, Trent pulled her closer, as close as he dared, surprised when she did not pull away, did not fight him. Holding her gaze, he kept his hand firmly on her back, the tips of his fingers gently tracing along her spine.

At his touch, she inhaled a sharp breath and sank her teeth into her lower lip as her back seemed to arch of its own volition. "Stop," she whispered almost pleadingly.

Lowering his head, Trent held her gaze. "Why?" When she did not answer, he asked, "What is it you hope for in a husband?"

Instantly, her eyes narrowed, and yet, the anger that flashed in them was only a mild echo of what he had seen before. "He shouldn't have told you," she whispered, for the first time averting her gaze.

"He's my friend," Trent replied, surprised by the seriousness of their conversation. "You're his sister. He wants us to be happy."

A deep frown drew down her brows. "Us?" Before Trent could reply, realisation came to her eyes and she immediately began to struggle in his arms. "I asked him to assist me in finding a husband," she prattled, her gaze fixed on something beyond his shoulder as though she did not dare meet his eyes. "As I cannot turn to my parents for help, I thought he would be the logical choice. He promised to take this seriously, to find me a suitable match, someone to share my interests, my fundamental characteristics, my—"

"What about love?" Trent interrupted, and she immediately

stilled in his arms, her gaze flying up to meet his. "And passion?" He inhaled deeply, tightening his hold on her, willing her to see how much she meant to him.

In answer, her muscles tensed, straining to get away. "You ought not speak of such things," she snapped, yet her voice lacked strength. "Release me. This does not concern you."

Belatedly realising that the music had come to an end, Trent refused to let her slip away. Holding on to her, he lowered his head, his gaze trapping hers. "You concern me," he whispered. "You always have…and you always will."

Thunderstruck, she stared up at him until they both sensed someone's approach.

Releasing her from his embrace, Trent looked up and found a rather stocky, young gentleman standing beside them, his pale blue eyes drifting from him to Winifred. "My lady, may I have this dance?"

Winifred swallowed, her lashes fluttering rapidly as she sought to regain her composure. "Certainly, my lord," she croaked and allowed him to pull her arm through his. Then she walked away, not even glancing over her shoulder.

Still, Trent could not help the warmth of hope from spreading into every fibre of his being. If he was not thoroughly mistaken—and he would wager his heart and soul that he was not!—then Winifred did care for him! He almost fainted in relief at the realisation.

However, she seemed afraid—terrified even!—at the thought of venturing away from her path of rational thought and sensible planning. Yes, they were not compatible in the strictest sense. They bickered and snapped at each other, baited the other and found joy in teasing one another beyond compare.

Still, Trent had no doubt that she was his other half, and he would not allow anyone else to claim her.

Sensible suitors be damned!

5

THE WRONG MAN

With the beginning of the new season, Winifred found herself in a carriage traveling toward London. Across from her, Griffin sat slumped in his seat, a stack of papers on his lap, from which he picked up one here and there, held it up to his face, read the notes he had scribbled on it before shifting his attention to the next.

"What are you doing?" Winifred enquired. Never in her life had she seen her brother so devoted to a piece of paper. For all intents and purposes, Griffin was a man of few intellectual interests, at least not those that required him to spend considerable time with pen and paper.

"Excuse me?" A frown on his face, he looked up, saw the confused expression on her face and sat up, straightening his shoulders with a moan. "Hell, my back hurts. Has this carriage always been this uncomfortable?"

"I suggest you change your posture. Now, what is this about?" Gesturing to the stack of papers, she turned questioning eyes to him.

For a moment he frowned, his gaze shifting back and forth between her and the papers on his lap as though the answer should be obvious. "In case you haven't noticed—which I see that you haven't!—I have spent the past fortnight cataloguing potential suitors to the best of my abilities." At her open-mouthed shock, he raised his eyebrows with a touch of haughtiness. "Indeed, after our five-year absence, instead of acquainting myself better with the *ladies* of the ton, I've done nothing but scribble down all those little details I know you think are important about the attending gentlemen at the New Year's ball at Stanhope Grove. There. Happy?"

Unable to form a coherent thought, Winifred stared at her brother. "Thank you," she whispered after a while, feeling tears sting the back of her eyes. "You really do love me, don't you?"

All teasing left Griffin's face as he saw the emotion in her eyes and a large smile claimed his lips. "Most fiercely," he whispered before he swallowed the lump that seemed to have settled in his own throat and held up one of the papers. "Here, I've listed their interests as well as characteristics I've become aware of during the ball. Now that the new season has begun, there will be plenty of opportunity to mingle. Once I narrow down my list, I shall see to it that you can meet the more suitable gentlemen in a more private setting, say a dinner party and the like. Seeing you interact with them will give me a better idea of who would suit you the most. Do you have any objections?"

Winifred shook her head. He had taken her seriously after all! Who would have guessed? After seeing him dancing with that fair-haired beauty, Winifred had assumed he had all but forgotten about his promise. How wrong she had been! "Thank you so much for doing this, Griffin. I know this is not easy for you."

A strained snort escaped him, and for a moment, he rubbed his hands over his face. "That's quite the understatement. To tell you the truth, I've never been more scared in my life."

Winifred frowned. "What do you mean?"

Griffin swallowed, turning serious eyes to her. "You trust me with your life, your future, your happiness. I'm afraid I'll make a mistake. I'm afraid because of me you will end up with the wrong man." He inhaled deeply. "I promise I shall do my utmost to ensure that that doesn't happen." Then with a last smile, he turned his attention back to the notes on the paper before him.

The wrong man? Winifred thought as—unbidden—Trent's dark green eyes flashed before her inner eye. Although she had tried to banish him from her thoughts for the past fortnight, he refused to release her. Remembering the way he had held her during their second dance still sent shivers down her spine, and she found herself closing her eyes, enjoying the memory of his touch.

The way he had held her had made her feel safe as though he would not hesitate to move mountains to protect her. Still, the way his hands had travelled over her back had also sent her heart into an uproar. She could still see the way his gaze had burnt into hers and hear his whispered words in her ear. *You concern me. You always have...and you always will.*

He had seemed so possessive of her during that dance, not at all like the Trent who always teased her, always called her *Fred*. For a moment—a short moment—it had almost seemed as though he had wanted to kiss her.

Winifred's body hummed with the memory of that feeling. *And passion?* He had asked. Was that what she had felt?

Shocked at the boldness of her thoughts, Winifred jerked her eyes open, trying to shake herself out of her daydreaming. Reminding herself that infatuations were always short-lived, she directed her gaze out the window, gazing at the passing landscape.

Infatuation? She frowned, realising the implication of her thoughts. At what point had she become...infatuated with Trent? Or was it not true? Had it only been the heat of the moment? Would she still feel the way she did now the next time she laid eyes on him?

Gritting her teeth, Winifred determinedly pushed that thought away. There was no need for her to see him outside of social events. After all, she had a future husband to find. Someone who suited her beyond the spur of the moment. Someone she could share her life with. Someone who understood her.

And that someone was certainly not Trent Henwood, Earl of Chadwick.

At least, she told herself so.

Sitting in the conservatory Griffin had added to their London townhouse for the sole reason of his sister's desire to paint, Winifred was engrossed in the glowing orchid slowly taking form on the canvas before her.

Her eyes shifted to the side, gazing at the live plant, trying to catch the way the afternoon light streamed in through the glass walls around her and set it aglow, giving it an otherwordly touch. The golden light almost seemed to dance on the snow-white petals, and Winifred sighed at the peaceful scene before her.

After the rather tumultuous beginning of the year, Winifred had spent the past few days locked away in a world of colours and light where the outcome of a painting was controlled by her skill alone. Nothing more. There were no contradicting emotions.

No misunderstood meanings.

No uncertainties.

"Ah, there you are."

Looking over her shoulder, she found her brother standing in the doorway, dressed to go out. "I've been here every day for the past few days," she reminded him, her brows raised in challenge. "If that fact has escaped your attention until now, I feel compelled to question your ability to assist me in choosing a suitable husband for you seem far from observant."

Grinning, Griffin approached. "Are you daring me to quit, dear Sister?"

Winifred swallowed, keeping a careful smile fixed on her face.

"Are you afraid I will choose poorly? Or are you reconsidering the requirements you placed on this endeavour?"

Setting down her paintbrush to have a reason to avert her gaze momentarily, Winifred rose from the stool. Then she took a step toward her brother. "Have you ever known me to change my mind?" she asked, her voice betraying a strength she did not feel.

"Not lightly."

"And I shall not do so now." Turning her gaze back to the window, Winifred felt her hands begin to tremble. Did she have doubts? She did not dare entertain that thought. For if she did and it turned out that it was true, what would she do then? What about her carefully forged plans? What would she do without them?

"I shall be out for the rest of the afternoon," Griffin said, his footsteps retreating toward the door before they stopped, and he took a few steps back. "By the way, your painting is beautiful. However, I must say I've seen similar ones all my life. Why do you never paint people?"

With her gaze fixed on the canvas, Winifred shrugged. "They're too complicated. There is no one way to paint someone. No right way.

I never know what to include and what not, how to…" Again, she shrugged, unable to put into words how people tended to confuse her. "They're not rational."

Griffin grinned. "I know. That's the beauty of it." Then his footsteps retreated once more. "Oh, I almost forgot. Trent will be over shortly; however, I won't be able to receive him."

As her heart hammered in her chest, Winifred turned toward her brother.

"You don't mind entertaining him, do you?"

"Me?" Winifred stammered, her hands gripping the paintbrush a bit too tightly. "Why can't you cancel on him?"

"Because he's already on his way."

"Then cancel your other plans." Her voice sounded almost pleading to her own ears.

Watching her, Griffin took a step closer, his brows drawn down. "If I didn't know any better, I'd think you didn't enjoy his company." A question lit up his eyes.

"How can I?" Winifred huffed, shaking her head at her brother. "He always teases me. He's insufferable."

Griffin chuckled, "I know. I like him, too." Then he turned to leave.

"What is so important that you cannot stay?" Winifred demanded, returning to the actual subject at hand.

"You."

"What?"

Stopping in the door frame, Griffin smiled. "I'm meeting a few *eligible bachelors* at White's."

Winifred's mouth dropped open. "You are? Why?"

Griffin sighed, "How can I judge their character if I don't know them?"

"Oh."

"Exactly." And with that, he turned and walked away, leaving her alone to face the one man who had always managed to turn her world upside down.

Trying to distract herself, Winifred turned her gaze back onto the canvas. However, the orchid failed to capture her attention. Despite Griffin's good intentions, she could not help but curse him for forcing this obligation on her. She could not simply send Trent away, or could she? Would that be in bad manners? After all, it was not she who had made plans with him. It had been her brother.

Feeling anger thudding through her veins, Winifred set down the image of the orchid she had been working on and retrieved a blank canvas. For a long moment, she stared at the white surface as it sat upon the easel, waiting to be filled with colour.

Snatching up her paintbrush, Winifred followed her intuition and quickly sketched her brother's face. Then she began to fill his image with life, giving his eyes a touch of mischief and his lips a curl of amusement. Before long, his portrait—although far from finished—had the same air of high-handedness about it which her brother always showed when doing what he thought right, ignoring others in the process.

It was a true likeness, one that captured his essence, and for the first time, Winifred felt satisfied with a portrait. Maybe once she had completed this one, she ought to try and paint others. Maybe it would help her understand people better.

All their layers.

All their—

"You truly have a talent."

Startled by Trent's voice only a few inches behind her, Winifred spun around, her paintbrush raised as though in defence, and before she knew what was happening the tip of her brush touched his face.

Shrinking back, she stared at the brown smudge on Trent's cheek. "I'm sorry. I didn't mean to…" Then she swallowed, and her gaze met his, taking note of the hint of surprise as well as the tickling amusement that painted a teasing smile on his face. "Have I not told you not to sneak up on a lady?" she snapped. "You're truly impossible!"

Laughing, he retrieved a handkerchief from his pocket and began wiping at the paint. "Oh, I'm impossible? You're the one to disfigure me, and I'm impossible?"

Winifred rolled her eyes, watching him spread the small smudge all over his cheek. "Oh, don't be so dramatic!" Then she stepped forward, "Give me this!" snatching the handkerchief from his hand. "You're making it worse."

He had the audacity to chuckle. "Why do I make you so nervous?"

Forcing her voice not to tremble, Winifred snapped, "You're not. You're mistaking annoyance for nervousness." Then she stepped back, and after dipping an edge of the handkerchief in a little fresh water she had set aside to clean her brushes, Winifred grabbed his chin rather roughly, turning his head sideways. "Now hold still or I swear I shall spread the paint all over your face."

Again, he chuckled as though nothing had ever been more amusing.

6

PASSION

Enthralled, Trent watched her as she began to wipe the paint off his cheek.

Her fingers held his chin tightly, and yet, they seemed to tremble ever so slightly as though the sudden contact had taken her off guard as much as him. Enjoying the feel of her touch as well as the warmth of her skin, Trent noticed her swallow when she caught him watching her, and he could not help but think that she felt something, too.

A woman unaffected did not look as she did, or did she?

Her eyes flicked back and forth between his own and the smudge on his face, and her cheeks seemed to darken with colour as though the emotions coursing through her at that moment ran deep. Still, despite her declaration to the contrary, she seemed nervous as though overwhelmed by their close contact.

"There," she finally said, releasing his chin and stepping back. "Now you look presentable again." Handing him back his handkerchief, she turned back to her painting, her gaze never quite meeting his.

Although Trent could not help but regret that the paint smudge had not been bigger and therefore more difficult to remove, he did not dare act on the impulse that coursed through his veins, urging him to reach for her and pull her into his arms. What would she do? Slap him? Scream?

No, before he did something so bold, he had to be certain of how she felt, of how she would react.

Looking over her shoulder, he tried to find something to say. "Since when do you paint people?"

"Since today."

Surprised, he took a step closer, feeling her stiffen as she straightened her back, the muscles in her jaw tense as she kept her gaze focused on the painting before them. "What brought on this change?" he asked, then chuckled. "Your brother I would presume, judging from the annoyingly superior look in his eyes."

At his words, he felt her relax slightly and a matching smile drew up the corners of her lips.

"What did he do?" Trent asked. "What made you paint him like this?"

The smile vanished from her face; however, she did not say a word.

"Have you ever painted me?" Trent prompted, wondering what her answer would have been if only she had shared it with him. Did it have something to do with him?

Turning her head, she looked at him, a slight frown drawing down her brows and a teasing curl coming to her lips. "Is your memory impaired somehow? Have you recently suffered a blow to the head?" When he frowned, she added, "Can you not recall what I just told you?"

Trent laughed, "I suppose I wasn't paying attention."

Rolling her eyes at him, she turned back to the painting. "To tell you the truth, few things you do surprise me."

He grinned, leaning in closer. "Would you care to elaborate?"

She inhaled a deep breath before stepping away and reaching for her paintbrush. "I'm afraid commenting on that would only make you more insufferable."

Again, he laughed, "Where's your brother?"

She stiffened but kept her gaze on the painting. "Out at White's. He asked me to make his apologies."

Confused for a split second, Trent nodded as he realised the significance of Griffin's absence. Judging from her evasiveness and how uncomfortable she felt in his presence, her brother was most likely working on their little *project* and trying to find her a suitable husband. Was there a deeper reason why she did not want him to know? Or was he simply imagining it?

Unable to help himself, he asked once more, "What do you look for in a husband?"

At his question, her hand tightened on the brush before she turned to look at him, her eyes narrowed, a warning resting in them. "Did I not tell you that this does not concern you?" She swallowed. "I'd much appreciate it if you would take your leave."

Trent swallowed, determined not to allow her to push him away. "Not until you answer me."

"Why?" she demanded, her eyes widening as they searched his face. "Why do you want to know? To tease me some more?"

"Do you not like it?" he asked, grinning, wondering how he had made it through the past five years without teasing her…without…her.

Again, her eyes narrowed. "Why would I? It's highly irritating." She stopped, and her gaze held his for a moment. "Do you?"

Closing the distance between them, Trent held her gaze, noticing the way she forced herself not to take a step back. "Very much so," he whispered, his breath touching her lips, making her shiver. "Now tell me, Fred, what is it you wish for in a husband?"

Swallowing, she held his gaze, determination shining in her eyes. "If you must know, I am hoping for a husband who does not tease me."

"Would that not be a dull life?" he teased as though by reflex, unable not to.

"Not at all." She shook her head. "It would be peaceful."

He frowned. "Peaceful or boring?"

Annoyed, she glared at him. "You're too much like my brother. You cannot take anything seriously." Shaking her head, she shrugged. "Why would you understand? You couldn't. But I…I want my life to be different. I want things to make sense." She inhaled a deep breath. "Griffin should not have told you."

"Why did you ask him for help? Why ask him to find you a husband?" Watching her face, Trent was not certain if he wanted to know. However, if he wanted to win her heart—and her hand—then he needed to know what she hoped for.

Sighing, she raised tired eyes to him. How often had she needed to explain herself? Trent wondered. "Because he knows me best. He knows who I am and what I need to be happy. Now that my parents are…" She swallowed, and he could see that their loss still haunted her. "He is the only one who can find me a suitable husband. Someone who's compatible with me."

Trent drew in a slow breath. "Griffin mentioned something like that."

"Then why did you ask me?" Winifred snapped, her gaze suddenly ablaze with anger. "Is this a new way to tease me? To annoy me?"

Not taking her bait, he held her gaze for a long moment, allowing the ensuing silence to soften her anger. "What about love and passion?"

As she inhaled a sharp breath, her eyelids began to flutter as though trying to hide her, to erase him from her vision. No doubt she remembered their dance at the New Year's ball, the way he had held her, touched her, whispered to her. Had that been her first taste of passion?

"Those…those aspects are of no importance," she stammered before she remembered to raise her chin and face him with those dark brown eyes full of quiet determination. "They are short-lived and no secure foundation for a life-long commitment."

Trent smiled. "Are you certain? Have you ever felt them?" Reaching out a hand, he brushed a stray lock from her face, gently tucking it behind her ear.

At his touch, she flinched. Still, for the barest of seconds, her eyes closed, and he could swear it was only her determination that made her take a step back.

"Why are you retreating from me?" he asked, his voice teasing, the look in his eyes far from it.

"I'm not."

"Then stand still." Holding her gaze, he once more closed the small distance between them. Her pulse in the side of her neck hammered wildly as he reached out to touch her hand. Gently, he brushed the tips of his fingers over her bare skin. At the ball, a layer of fabric had separated them as she had worn gloves. Now, however, the warmth of her skin called to him, and he entwined his fingers through hers, holding her hand in his.

As her chest rose and fell with her rapid breathing, Trent began to feel light-headed. Her gaze held his without wavering, and yet, there was still resistance in the way she stood before him.

"You should leave," she said, her voice almost pleading.

Why could she not simply admit that she felt something for him? "Why?"

"My brother is not here."

A teasing smile curled up the corners of his mouth. "I cannot say I mind for I enjoy spending time with you." His hand tightened on hers, and she drew in a sharp breath. "I've missed you."

Blinking, she stared at him as though she did not believe her ears. "It's been a long time."

He nodded.

"I meant to…I mean." She swallowed. "When my parents died, I was overwhelmed with grief and sorrow. I couldn't…"

Trent frowned. "What are you trying to say?"

She drew in a slow breath. "I never stopped to remember that you lost them, too. And then Griffin and I left and you…" She squeezed his hand. "You remained here all by yourself. I should have thought to…"

"To what?" he prompted, deeply affected by the way she had thought of him. Had he been on her mind every once in a while over the past five years? He could only hope so.

"To ask you to join us." For a moment, her eyes closed before a deep sadness and honest regret showed in them. "Ever since you first came to Atherton House with Griffin, you've been a part of our family. You belong with us…and then we forgot about you." Tears brimmed in the corners of her eyes as she looked at him, her gaze pleading with him to forgive her.

Trying to swallow the lump that had settled in his throat, Trent tried to sort through the renewed feelings of loss that assailed him. "Even if, I couldn't have come. I had responsi—"

"But I should have thought to ask!"

"Griffin did."

Her eyes widened. "He did?"

Trent nodded. "He asked me to come, and I wanted to, but after my father's death, there was too much I needed to handle. I simply couldn't."

Nodding, she held his gaze, her dark brown eyes full of emotion that he felt tempted to pull her into his arms. "I'm sorry," she whispered, once more squeezing his hand. "I'm so sorry."

"I know. As am I."

Silence stretched between them as they gazed at one another, remembering the life they had shared and the loss that had torn them apart. In a way, at their core, they were still the same, and yet, time had passed, changing something they could not quite grasp.

Swallowing, she pulled her hand from his...and reluctantly, he released her. "You should go," she said for the second time that day, the hint of a smile coming to her face as her eyes lit up with child-like mischief. "Even if my brother has no sense of propriety, I do. You should not be here when he is not."

Noting the change in the air as though the dark cloud had moved on, revealing the sun, Trent grinned at her. "You seem determined to get rid of me, dear Fred. Are you afraid I have untoward intentions?" Winking at her, he stepped closer.

A deep smile came to her face, relieving the tension that had held her, and she laughed. "Not at all. I am merely concerned for my reputation." She glanced at her half-finished painting. "Still, I could do with a little peace and quiet or my brother will never have a teasing likeness to hang over the mantle."

Chuckling, Trent inclined his head to her. "What a marvellous idea!" Then he stepped back and took his leave, relieved to feel the ease between them returning, knowing that now was not the right time to reveal to her what intentions he had...untoward or otherwise.

7

WALTZING WITH THE ENEMY

Over the course of the next few weeks, Winifred found that choosing a husband was quite time-consuming…at least if one did it right.

As the new season began and London reawakened, Winifred followed her brother from ball to ball, attended performances at Covent Garden and promenaded through Hyde Park. Due to their five-year absence, the ton seemed quite intrigued to have the Earl of Amberly and his sister back in their midst; after all, they both possessed assets that made them quiet desirable on the marriage market.

Dancing with a large number of eligible men—many of which were urged in her direction by overbearing mother's looking for a good match!—Winifred tried her best to discover who would suit her enough to be considered a potential husband. Although her intuition told her quite early whether she liked a gentleman or not, she urged herself not to draw hasty conclusions. After all, getting to know another's character could not be accomplished during one evening, let alone within a few minutes.

Her brother usually stood off to the side, alternately watching her and conversing with the gentlemen he deemed worthy of his sister's hand—quite to the disappointment of London's eligible ladies!

As Lord Haverton guided her across the dance floor, Winifred once more glanced over his shoulder and spotted her brother, politely but insistently extracting himself from a young lady's grasp. Smiling, Winifred sighed. He truly was most diligent in keeping his promise! She never would have expected him to do so, but it did warm her heart and reminded her of how much she meant to him!

"You seem amused," Lord Haverton observed, his kind green eyes gliding over her face. "It suits you."

Inclining her head at the compliment, Winifred considered how to reply. "My brother seems very…watchful this evening."

Lord Haverton smiled, and as they turned he glanced in Griffin's direction. "He does indeed." His green eyes returned to her. "He seems very protective of you, Lady Winifred. That speaks highly of him and you."

"Thank you, my lord." Smiling back at him, Winifred realised that she was enjoying his company quite a lot. He was a decent man, kind and considerate. He always spoke truthfully as his eyes never seemed to disagree with his words, and his smile betrayed a caring heart and respectful demeanour. Her brother had indeed done well when he had encouraged her to get better acquainted with Lord Haverton.

When the music stopped, her dance partner inclined his head to her. "Thank you for this dance, my lady." His green eyes held hers, and he seemed reluctant to take his leave. "I was wondering if—"

"May I have the next dance?"

Goose bumps raced down Winifred's spine at the sound of Trent's voice, and she turned to him wishing her face held more annoyance than she knew it did. Out of the corner of her eye, she noticed a touch of disappointment come to Lord Haverton's face. However, her attention instantly focused on the mirth twinkling in Trent's dark green gaze as he held out his hand to her.

"Or are you otherwise engaged?" he asked, the look in his eyes growing darker as though he dared her to refuse him.

"Not at present," Winifred heard herself say before turning back to Lord Haverton, thanking him for their dance. When he took his leave, Trent instantly drew her into his arms as the first notes of a waltz began to play.

Reminding herself to be annoyed with his overbearing attitude, Winifred stepped on his foot as hard as she dared without it being obvious to those around her.

Sucking in a sharp breath, Trent turned wide eyes to her. For a moment, he seemed taken aback. However, that moment was short-lived. His lips curled up in a smile, and his hand tightened on her back. "You did that on purpose," he accused, seemingly delighted with her actions.

"I did," Winifred admitted freely, trying to straighten her back lest she sink into his arms. "As did you."

A frown came to his face. His eyes, however, still held the same satisfied twinkle she had seen there before. "I'm afraid I do not know what you mean."

Winifred scoffed, "Don't play innocent, Trent. Every time a waltz is played, you appear as though out of nowhere." A frown drew down her brows. "How do you know? Do you have an acquaintance among the musicians? Are you clairvoyant?"

Laughing at the teasing note in her voice, Trent lowered his head to her conspiratorially. "I assure you, dear Fred, it is merely a coincidence."

Rolling her eyes at him, Winifred sighed, starting to feel annoyed. "Stop calling me that." She glanced around. "What if someone overhears you? What if others start—"

"Calling you Fred?"

She nodded.

His hands tightened on her, and the air flew from her lungs at the intensity in his gaze as he looked at her. "If they know what's best for them, they won't." He inhaled slowly, his gaze unwavering. "It's mine. Mine alone."

Staring up at him, Winifred could not help but think that he was saying a lot more than claiming her *nickname* as his. It was as though he was...claiming *her*...as his. Swallowing, Winifred averted her gaze, focusing her thoughts on the steps. Steps she knew in her sleep. Steps that provided little distraction from the man holding her in his arms.

"You seem quiet suddenly," he observed, a touch of concern in his dark green eyes. "Is something wrong?"

Winifred sighed, groping for something to say. "I am...merely concerned about Lord Haverton." Trent rolled his eyes. "The way you claimed this dance was quite rude as you did interrupt him. I don't even know what he wanted to say. I must go and apologise." Craning her neck, Winifred tried to spot the young lord among the sea of guests, glad to have somewhere to look but into Trent's disconcerting eyes.

"Is he the one?" he asked unexpectedly, his voice strained as though her answer would determine the course of his own life. "Have you made your choice?"

Winifred swallowed, carefully raising her eyes to his. What she saw there confused her as she could have sworn that—

"Have you?" Trent prompted impatiently, his jaw tense and his voice almost a growl.

Winifred swallowed. "What is it to you?"

His lips pressed into a thin line, and his gaze was hard as it held hers. "Answer me."

Winifred shrugged. "I have not." All the tension seemed to leave Trent's body. "However, I think we would suit each other. Still, it is too soon to tell."

Trent drew in a slow breath. "Good," was all he said, and when the music ended, he squeezed her hand one last time and then took his leave.

Still swaying from the effects of their dance, Winifred turned to her next dance partner, momentarily at a loss as to who he was.

Never would he have seen this coming!

8

A SENSIBLE MATCH

A few days later, Winifred found herself bundled up in her warmest winter clothes sitting next to Lord Haverton in his open chaise as they took a turn through Hyde Park. After apologising to him for Trent's rude behaviour, he had enquired if she would allow him to call on her. As Winifred had no reason to object, he had stopped by the following morning, accompanied by his mother, a woman who portrayed the evil witch with every fibre of her being.

Winifred had been more than relieved when they had left. Although she did come to care for the young lord, his mother was the making of nightmares. Ought she exclude him from consideration based on his family's attributes? It was a new thought that hadn't occurred to her before. However, if she were to marry Lord Haverton, his mother would become an important part of her life as well. Could she live with that?

"Do you prefer watercolours?" Lord Haverton asked, guiding the two horses pulling their chaise around a bend. "Or oil?"

"Watercolours."

"May I ask why?"

Winifred shrugged, wiggling her chilled fingers inside her muff. "I dislike the smell of oil colours."

Lord Haverton nodded. "I agree. Painting is a very sensory activity. One ought to reduce negative influences as much as possible." Glancing at her, he smiled. "Would you allow me to see your paintings?"

"Certainly, my lord. I've never thought to hide them. You're welcome to visit and take a look."

"I shall."

As they came around a small grove, the Serpentine appeared before them, its waters glistening in the brilliant sun as it gave a magical glow to everything it touched. "What a magnificent sight!" Lord Haverton exclaimed. "I admit I am fascinated by the influence of light on everyday objects. It often seems to change how things appear. The lake, for instance, seems almost mystical in the sunlight. However, in its absence, the waters often appear murky as though danger awaited."

"I agree." Feeling eagerness course through her veins, Winifred gazed at the lake, remembering the orchid she had painted a few weeks ago. "When I paint in the conservatory, I can paint the same objects, but always have it appear differently depending on the time of day. It is truly fascinating."

Again, Lord Haverton smiled at her, and Winifred could see that he was as pleased with their conversation as she was. Indeed, they had a lot in common and his disposition suited her. He never riled her, but instead was always attentive, always considerate. His smile was warm and affecting, and his green eyes held warmth and kindness.

Still, sometimes when she looked at them, Winifred could not help but see another pair of green eyes in her mind. Dark green to be exact, with a wicked gleam in them.

"Good afternoon, Lady Wini*fred*, Lord Haverton."

At the sound of his voice, Winifred closed her eyes for the barest of seconds, wondering if her thoughts had called him here. Why was it that he always knew where she was? Why did he always follow? It was quite aggravating, and from the way Lord Haverton's lips thinned, he did not care for the interruption, either.

Turning toward approaching hoof beats, Winifred balled her hands inside her muff into fists, willing Trent to simply greet them and leave. However, judging from the look on his face, he seemed disinclined to be agreeable.

"Good day, Lord Chadwick," Lord Haverton greeted their unwelcome acquaintance. "It is a beautiful day, is it not?"

"It is indeed." Sitting atop his black gelding, Trent barely looked at Winifred's companion as his dark gaze seemed focused on her. Still, he spoke politely as though their meeting had come about entirely by chance. Knowing Trent, Winifred was certain that chance had had no hand in this.

"What brings you here?" she enquired as uncomfortable silence began to linger in the air.

Trent merely shrugged. His shoulders, however, seemed tense, and he gripped the reins rather tightly. Did something bother him? "After last night's festivities, I had merely hoped for some fresh air." He swallowed, and his gaze met hers once again. "To clear my head."

After a little more uncomfortable and rather meaningless chitchat, Trent took his leave and they went their separate ways. Relieved, Winifred allowed Lord Haverton to take her home, accepting his invitation to have tea with him and his mother sometime soon.

Strangely exhausted, Winifred went up to her room and rested for an hour or two before heading back downstairs to the conservatory. If there were ever a place that had the power to soothe her raging emotions, it was the small glass pavilion. Although it was late afternoon, the sun streamed in, setting everything aglow, and the myriad of flowers beckoned her forward, their scents, sweet and engaging, promising better days. Easier days.

Putting the final touches on her brother's portrait, Winifred felt her muscles relax and before long a smile drew up the corners of her mouth. Despite Trent's interruption, it had been a pleasant day. After all, it had allowed her a deeper glimpse at Lord Haverton's character. He was indeed the kind of man she had been looking for. He would make her a good husband, would he not? Would she make him a good wife? Ought she to make her choice? Or was that premature?

As footsteps echoed closer, Winifred stepped back from the easel. "Griffin, what do you think? Would you say this is a fitting likeness?"

"I would indeed," Trent spoke from behind her, and she whirled around.

"What are you doing here?" Winifred demanded as the cloud of peaceful tranquility that had engulfed her only a moment ago slowly evaporated. "My brother is not here."

Grinning from ear to ear, Trent stopped in front of her. "I

know. I came to enquire after your morning with Lord Haverton."

At his frank admission, Winifred's mouth fell slightly open. "You have no right to ask such a question."

"I know. I'll ask it nonetheless." His gaze held hers, daring her to answer.

Winifred swallowed before stepping sideways to set down her paintbrush, thus giving her a reason to avert her eyes. "However, I will not answer." Lifting her gaze to his, she squared her shoulders. "I need to ask you to leave. It is not proper for you to be here when my brother is not."

A challenging gleam came to his eyes as he stepped closer. "You were out alone with Lord Haverton," he observed, a touch of an accusation in his voice.

"Yes, we were out in the open," Winifred retorted, annoyed with his overbearing attitude. Who did he think he was? Her brother? "For everyone to see. We, however," she gestured to the two of them, "are alone."

At her last word, a spark seemed to light up his eyes, and Winifred felt her courage falter. Swallowing, she took a step back before glancing over Trent's shoulder, wishing her brother were here. How dare he leave them alone together?

As though he had read her thoughts, Trent took a step closer, unwilling to allow her to escape. A wicked smile curled up his lips, and his eyes teased her. "Are you afraid I have untoward intentions?" he asked as he had before.

Winifred rolled her eyes, knowing that the best way to deal with Trent's affinity for mockery was to not take him seriously.

His eyes searched her face, and an amused smile came to his own. "You do not believe it possible, do you?" he asked, then shook his head. "Perhaps you're right. Perhaps I should go. Perhaps it is not safe for you to be alone with me."

Unable to hide her surprise at his admission, Winifred frowned, trying to make sense of this change in attitude. Deep down, there was a part of her that doubted that he was merely teasing her.

Holding her gaze, Trent leaned his head down to her. "I don't mean to frighten you, dear Fred, but I thought you should know."

Winifred swallowed. "Know what?"

A teasing grin came to Trent's face. Still, his gaze remained serious. "That I have untoward intentions."

9

UNTOWARD INTENTIONS

Seeing the understanding on her face, Trent fought to resist the urge to pull her into his arms and show her that she was his and would never be Haverton's. When he had heard about their outing from Griffin, his insides had twisted painfully, and he had not been able to keep himself from going to find them. As predicted, it had taken all his willpower to not throttle Haverton, but instead allow Winifred to leave with him.

Never in his life had he found himself in a more trying situation.

Now, finding the woman he loved only an arm's length away from him, her wide eyes fixed on his, her chest rising and falling with each rapid breath, Trent wondered what she would say if he were to kiss her. Would she reject him?

His teeth clenched. Would she reject Haverton?

Feeling his own nerves flutter, Trent glimpsed the paintbrush she had set down a few minutes ago. Instantly, it brought back the memory of a few weeks ago when she had accidentally gotten paint on his cheek. He remembered her closeness, her touch, her warmth, and a deep longing rose inside him.

Flashing a teasing grin at her, he leaned forward, noting the way she in turn leaned back and drew in a sharp breath, before he reached for the abandoned paintbrush. Straightening, he held her gaze, then quickly brought up the brush and in one fluid motion drew it across her cheek, leaving a trail of black paint. "Quite untoward, I assure you," he laughed, delighted when her eyes widened in outrage.

Shrieking, she slapped his hand away, her own touching her cheek. Then she brought it before her eyes, which widened even more when she saw the black smudge on her fingertips. "How dare you?" she demanded, her eyes ablaze with sudden fury.

Smiling, Trent could not bring himself to feel remorse. After all, it was that fire in her that he loved most. He could never live a life without teasing her. Could she?

Before he knew what was happening, she threw herself at him like a wild fury, snatching the brush from his grasp and attacking him with equal measure. The brush still moist with paint surged toward him, and only in the last instant did he manage to sidestep her attack.

Turning on her heel, she came after him again. "You'll regret this!" she snarled, once more raising her arm, once more aiming the brush at his face.

Laughing, Trent turned, then to his surprise managed to grasp her wrist, the tip of the brush only a hair's breadth from his skin. "Dear Fred, be *sensible*," he teased, delighting in the way her jaw clenched and she growled at him.

As they struggled, he managed to twist the brush from her grip and tossed it across the floor where it came to rest next to a large flowerpot at a safe distance. With the weapon disposed of, he slipped an arm around her waist and pulled her against him, noting with satisfaction the widening of her eyes as her hands stilled. "I never knew you had such passion within you," he whispered. "Or perhaps I did know." Then he grasped her chin—the way she had grasped his—and tilted her head upward, her lips only a hair's breadth away from his own. "Did you kiss Haverton?"

Her eyes grew round—whether at his question or their closeness he did not know—before she pressed her lips into a thin line, glaring at him. Still, she did not try to free herself from his grasp. "That would have been highly improper," she spat as though her words were an insult to him.

Quite on the contrary. Trent felt his muscles relax, finally free to enjoy holding her in his arms...and away from prying eyes no less. Whenever he had swept her into a waltz over the past few weeks—vowing to never allow another man to hold her in his arms—he had been tempted to kiss her more than once. However, with the ton watching that had never been an option.

Now, however, things were different.

"Did you want to?" he pressed, noting the way her long lashes fluttered up and down.

Opening her mouth to reply, she stopped, staring at him for a long moment. Then she straightened her spine, trying to free herself from his grip.

"Answer me," Trent demanded, tightening his hold on her.

A slight blush crept into her cheeks, and Trent felt his insides burn with jealousy. "I can't say," she finally whispered, her gaze lifted defiantly. "I hadn't thought about it."

Once more, Trent felt himself relax with relief. "Then you didn't," he concluded, elaborating when he saw the soft frown on her face. "If you had, nothing could have stopped you from thinking about it."

For a moment her gaze remained on his before she abruptly dropped it, a deep flush coming to her face, and tried to free herself from his grasp once more.

Trent felt his breath get stuck in his throat as hope surged through him. "Are you thinking about kissing me?" he asked boldly, and her head snapped up as though he had struck her.

10

BEING NONSENSICAL

As her cheeks burnt with embarrassment, Winifred stared up into Trent's face, his gaze searching hers. Could he read her thoughts in her eyes? Did he know? Suspect?

Cursing herself, Winifred did not know what had brought on these sudden desires. Why was it that he was the one person who made her feel this way? The one person that made her act and feel like a silly girl? Uncertain? Not in control?

Steeling herself against the tantalising touch of his fingers on her skin, the way his strong arm held her pressed to his body, Winifred lifted her hands and in one fluid motion pushed him away. "Don't be ridiculous," she snapped–or tried to–as she turned back to the painting behind her, hoping to hide the uncertainty and temptation that all too likely showed on her face.

"I don't believe I am," he replied, the tone in his voice daring her to turn and face him. "I believe you're afraid."

Whirling around, determined to put him in his place once and for all, Winifred opened her mouth in outrage. "Afraid of wh–?"

Suddenly, he was there, right in front of her, barely a hair's breadth away. Pulling her back into his arms, he brushed his knuckles along the line of her jaw before his hand came to rest on the back of her neck. "Of being nonsensical," he answered her outburst before his mouth closed over hers.

In an instant, logic and reason and sense went out the window as emotions long held in check surged to the forefront. Although shock froze her limbs for a few moments, Winifred could not deny the all-consuming warmth that swept through her.

As he held her in his arms, his lips teasing her to follow him down this path, Winifred felt herself respond without thought. Something other than her rational mind urged her on, and she did not have the strength to resist.

Returning his kiss with equal measure, Winifred wondered at her own boldness. Still, when his tongue met hers, even that last thought disappeared into thin air as though it had never been.

After wrenching his lips from hers, Trent whispered, "I've been wanting to do that for a long time, Fred. A very long time."

Staring up at him, Winifred tried to sort through the tumult in her heart. His gaze held hers, and his eyes shone with such intensity as she had never seen them. Deep emotions rested in them, and from one moment to the next, Winifred understood…everything.

Why he had demanded every waltz.

Why he had glared at Haverton.

Why he called her Fred.

And yet, it could not be. It simply could not.

Panic began to well up in her chest as her heart and mind locked in battle. What was she to do? What was the right course of action?

Oh, how she wished her mother were here!

Instead, it was Griffin who suddenly stood in the doorway, clearing his throat.

Startled, they both flinched, whirling around to face the unexpected interruption.

With the touch of a smirk on his face, her brother looked from her to Trent. "Care to explain what is going on here?"

Meeting her eyes, Trent nodded. Then his hand grasped hers, and he took a step forward. "Griffin, I apologise," he began, and in that moment, Winifred knew exactly what he would say. "However, I—"

"You need to go," she interrupted, pulling her hand from his. "I need to speak to my brother."

Turning to look at her, his eyes narrowed, and she could see his confusion only too plainly on his face. "But I—"

"No!" Shaking her head, she looked at him, hoping he could forgive her. But she was not ready for this. She simply was not.

Within a matter of minutes, her entire world had shifted, turned upside down, and she was in no state of mind to make a life-altering decision here and now.

Her heart ached as she saw pain and disappointment well up in his eyes. Still, he nodded. "If this is what you want, I will go," he forced out. Then, however, he took a step closer and whispered, "But I will not walk away." His gaze burnt into hers. "You belong with me as I belong with you. No amount of sensible reasoning can change that." Then he turned, nodded at Griffin and disappeared.

As though she had held her breath, her lungs began to burn, and she gulped down a few deep breaths, trying to steady her trembling hands.

"Are you all right?" Griffin asked, a bit of a smirk on his face. When she nodded, his smile grew wider. "And are you aware that he was just about to ask for your hand?"

"I'm not an idiot!" Winifred snapped, taken aback by the harshness in her voice.

Griffin laughed, "Well, to tell you the truth, dear Sister, you've been acting like one."

Instantly, her head jerked around, and she stared at her brother. "This is all your fault!" she hissed as sudden light-headedness engulfed her. "You shouldn't have left us alone. You should've been here. If you had, he would never have…"

"Kissed you?" Griffin prompted, his face suddenly serious. "Whether you want to believe it or not, whether you like it or not doesn't matter, but he has been in love with you for a very long time." Gently, he took her hand. "Only today he finally had the courage to express how he felt."

Gritting her teeth, Winifred shook her head. "It doesn't matter. I know what I want. I told you, and I thought you were willing to take this seriously, to help me." Searching his gaze, she swallowed. "And you did, didn't you? You suggested Lord Haverton, and you were right. He suits me. He does."

A deep frown came to Griffin's face. "I do not deny that. But…" Squeezing her hands, he held her gaze. "Do you truly not care

about love? You may be suited to Haverton, but do you love him?"

Bowing her head, Winifred stepped back, pulling her hands out of her brother's grasp. Her heart ached, and her mind buzzed like a beehive. She could not think, and she had no clue how she felt.

Inhaling a deep breath, Griffin took a step back, giving her space. "I apologise for upsetting you. It was never my intention. However, I do hope that you think long and hard about what you truly want. Nevertheless, it is your decision." He turned to go, but then stopped in the doorway. "I actually came to tell you that Eleanor is here. We ran into each other on the front stoop upon my return from White's. She's waiting in the drawing room." A moment of silence hung in the air. "Perhaps you should speak to her." Then he turned and walked away.

Gritting her teeth against the shivers that wrecked her body, Winifred tried her best to gain control of her fluttering nerves. Never in her life had she felt as much at the mercy of her treacherous heart as now. Well, maybe when her parents had died.

Still, who would ever choose to feel like this? And if she chose Trent, if she trusted his words, then he would have the power to make her feel like this whenever he chose.

No. The more sensible course of action was to forget today had ever happened and go back to the way things were.

Inhaling a deep breath, Winifred wiped the paint smudge from her cheek, brushed her hands over her dress, tugged away a stray curl and forced a pleasant smile on her face. Then she left the conservatory and headed to the drawing room to greet Eleanor, determined to pass a pleasant afternoon chatting with her friend.

However, the moment she entered the drawing room, Eleanor's eyes narrowed. Her joyous smile momentarily froze on her lips before she stepped forward, her gaze searching Winifred's face. "What happened?"

Winifred swallowed, willing the corners of her mouth to remain where they were. "Nothing," she lied, stepping around her friend and gesturing for her to take a seat, all the while keeping her eyes firmly fixed on anything but the woman eyeing her with unconcealed concern. "Merely an argument with my brother. He can be quite tiresome at times. Would you care for some tea?"

Eleanor drew in a deep breath, her gaze shifting sideways as though she were contemplating what to say. "My dear Winifred," she began, and even then, Winifred knew that she had lost. "You're one of my oldest and most trusted friends. I admit we haven't seen each other for quite some time and I'm certain I know you less now than I did then. However, even a fool could see that your heart is aching most acutely." A gentle smile came to her lips. Her eyes, however, still held the same determination. "Tell me what happened. Is it Lord Chadwick?"

Winifred froze, her eyes wide, staring at her friend. "How do you...?"

Eleanor chuckled, "Because you love him, and because he loves you." Reaching out, she grasped Winifred's hand. "What happened?"

Winifred swallowed. Perhaps her brother was right. Perhaps she ought to tell Eleanor. After all, she was a woman and perhaps she could advise her in a way her brother simply could not. "He kissed me," she finally admitted, noticing the delight in her friend's gaze. "And I believe he...was about to ask for my hand."

"Was about to?" Eleanor frowned. "What stopped him?"

"I did." Pulling her hand from Eleanor's grasp, Winifred rose to her feet, suddenly unable to remain still. "I could see it on his face, and...and I panicked." Turning to look at Eleanor, she shook her head. "I started to feel light-headed. I..."

"The thought of him proposing frightened you?" Eleanor asked, stepping toward her, her kind eyes suggesting that she tried to understand. "Why?"

"Because we are not suited to one another!" Winifred huffed, feeling overwhelmed by the constant need to explain herself.

"How do you know?" Eleanor demanded before a teasing twinkle came to her eyes. "Did you not enjoy his kiss?"

For a long moment, Winifred stared at her friend, not knowing what to say.

"Why can you not admit that you care about him?" Eleanor asked, a frown coming to her face. "I can see that you do. He means a lot to you. He always has."

Winifred shrugged, trying her best to understand and in turn explain it to Eleanor. "We grew up together. He's like a brother to me."

Eleanor laughed, "He most certainly is not. I've told you before that he does not look at you as a brother does and neither do you look at him as you do Griffin. What you feel for him is different, believe me."

"Even if it is," Winifred conceded. "It is only a momentary infatuation. It will not last, and when it ends, I'll be stuck with a man whose favourite pastime it is to tease me, to mock me, to call me names. How is that a good foundation for a marriage?"

Stepping forward, Eleanor once more drew Winifred's hands into her own, her kind eyes meeting her friend's. "Look at me, Winifred. Do you truly dislike his teasing? Ask yourself honestly if you would wish for him to stop. How would you feel if he were to never again call you Fred? Do you truly believe it to be an insult?"

Remembering the many times Trent had called her Fred, Winifred knew that it was not. For whenever he had, his eyes had shone brightly with affection, with fondness, with tenderness. When they had danced, he had told her that his nickname for her was his…his alone, and no one else was to use it. He would see to that. "I do not," she finally admitted, feeling as though Eleanor had just robbed her of her one good reason not to give in, not to be swayed from her chosen path.

Squeezing Winifred's hands gently, Eleanor smiled at her. "I always thought it sounded like a term of endearment, and he's used it for years, has he not?" Winifred nodded. "To me, that means that you've been in his heart for a very long time. There is nothing momentary about how he feels about you."

Winifred sighed, remembering Trent's intense gaze as he had told her that he's been wanting to kiss her for a very long time. Had he been truthful? Never had he lied to her. There was no good reason not to believe him.

Still, now that her mother was dead, Winifred could not bring herself to sway from the path she knew her mother would have approved of. Would it not be a betrayal? Would she feel as though she'd lost her mother all over again? As strange as it was, following in her mother's footsteps had made her feel closer to the woman who had walked by her side all her life. And although she was not a little girl any longer, Winifred was not certain if she was ready to face life alone.

On her own.

What ought she to do?

11

A HAPPY COUPLE

A mere two days later, Trent found himself at yet another ball, his hands painfully wrapped around a glass as he stared across the dance floor, watching the woman he loved dance with the man she wished to marry. How had they reached this point?

Only two days ago, he had been on the verge of asking for her hand...and then she had stopped him, her eyes wide with panic. Why did she not want to marry him? Did she not care for him? However, the way she had responded to his kiss had suggested otherwise. In the moment her lips had melted against his own, he had felt certain of her affections, of her acceptance of his proposal, of a shared future.

Now, it seemed as far-fetched as snow in July.

Watching as the *happy couple* strolled off the dance floor, Trent gritted his teeth against the bile rising in his throat. How could he simply stand here and allow Lord Haverton to court *his* Fred? Still, he had to admit that it was her choice. As much as he wanted to rush over and pound the other man into the ground, it would not change that it was her choice. Quite on the contrary, such a reaction would probably convince her that he was not the right man for her for good. But what else could he do? Was he simply to stand here and watch?

"How are you doing?" Griffin asked, stepping up next to him, his gaze shifting from Trent's face to the *happy couple* down by the refreshment table. "You seem rather ill at ease, my friend."

Trent scoffed. What an understatement! "Did you come here to mock me?"

"Not at all." Grinning from ear to ear, Griffin asked, "Do you have a plan? I mean besides sulking in the corner and glaring at the man who will steal the woman you love from under your nose if you're not careful?"

Exhaling loudly, Trent turned his dark stare on his friend. "What do you suggest I do? Your sister has made it very clear that she does not wish to marry me."

Shaking his head, Griffin sighed.

In that moment, Trent could have settled for pounding his friend into the ground. Why was he making this even harder than it already was?

"You know," Griffin began, his voice suddenly casual, "given the circumstances I found the two of you in a few days ago, my sister might be persuaded to marry you to avoid a scandal."

Trent snorted, "You know very well that I would never force myself on your sister. In addition, she would never bend her will to anyone," he sighed, "which is one of the reasons I love her."

Griffin grinned, deep pleasure in his eyes. "That's all I wanted to hear, my friend." Jovially, he clapped Trent on the shoulder. "However, you're wrong in one regard."

"And what is that?"

"She is currently bending her will to the ludicrous notion that love and compatibility are mutually exclusive." He shrugged. "Don't ask me how she came to that conclusion. I believe it has something to do with how our parents came to be married. Still, it's a twisted reason for choosing a husband, and I fear that one day she will wake up and realise that she sacrificed her own happiness for the approval of a ghost."

Griffin's words brought back the memory of a cold December afternoon over a decade ago when a young Winifred, barely thirteen years old at the time, had spoken to him quite vehemently of the merits of matching dispositions. That day, her example had been her brother's rather wild and carefree character in contrast to her own more sensible and considerate disposition. She had pointed out how—due to their differences—they would never get along and that she would eternally be burdened with a brother whom she could not understand, leaving them forever in a state of constant aggravation.

Still, was there anyone closer to her today than her brother? Had they not bonded over their shared loss? Was there anyone else she trusted more? After all, she had asked him to choose her future husband. Did that not speak of unwavering trust?

"Have you told her how you feel?" Griffin asked, watchful eyes focused on Trent's face.

"Certainly, I hav—" Breaking off mid-sentence, Trent realised that although he had finally admitted his feelings for Winifred to himself, he had never spoken the very words out loud. Not to her. Not to the one person who needed to know. "I did not," he mumbled, wondering how he could have overlooked such an important detail. "I thought I had made it clear, but I've never actually told her that I love her."

"Don't you think you should," Griffin asked, a touch of amusement in his voice, "before you admit defeat? Even if for an objective observer there is no mistaking your feelings for her, hearing it out loud might help her realise what she is about to give up. Perhaps she simply needs to hear it."

Watching Winifred walk away on Haverton's arm, Trent drew in a deep breath. "What if I'm fooling myself?" He turned to look at his friend. "What if she simply doesn't care for me?"

Griffin frowned. "Then why doesn't she simply tell you? I bet to this day she's never said anything like that to you, has she?"

Trent shook his head. "Perhaps she is only trying to spare my feelings."

Laughing, Griffin stepped closer, placing an encouraging hand on Trent's shoulder. "Listen, from where I stand it seems that she is doing her utmost to keep herself distracted, and there's only one reason a woman would do so."

Feeling his hands tremble, Trent looked at his friend, eagerly awaiting his answer. "Which is?"

Griffin sighed as though all of this was obvious and Trent a fool for not realising it on his own. "Because she's afraid of what she truly wants."

Trent swallowed as treacherous hope swelled in his chest. Lifting his gaze, he looked around. However, the spot by the refreshment table was now occupied by another couple. Where had they gone? What if Haverton proposed to Winifred in this very moment? What if she accepted him? "I need to find her," Trent declared as his heart thudded wildly in his chest, terrified at the thought that he had lost his chance.

A satisfied smile on his face, Griffin nodded. "I'll help you."

12

NO REASONABLE OBJECTION

"These orchids are beautiful," Winifred exclaimed as they strolled through the conservatory, its glass walls making them visible to the attending guests in the ballroom. Engrossed, her gaze shifted from one flower to the next. "I would love to see them during the day with the sun shining in."

Lord Haverton nodded. "I would certainly love to see you paint them. I so admire your ability to capture their beauty. I myself am doomed to admire as I cannot create myself." Despite his words, a delighted smile rested on his face and he looked at her with the greatest admiration shining in his kind green eyes.

Eyes that—unfortunately—reminded her of another man!

Chiding herself for the direction of her thoughts, Winifred lifted her gaze and smiled at the man who had been attentive to her all throughout the evening. She could not deny that he was a kind and decent man and that their conversation was quite stimulating, bringing her great joy as well as peace of mind. On top of that, he was a handsome man with chestnut brown hair and startling green eyes that never failed to light up whenever he saw her.

Did you want to kiss him? Unbidden, Trent's question echoed in her mind, and Winifred could not deny that…she did not. Or did she? How was she to know? Perhaps she had to kiss him before knowing that she wanted more kisses? Perhaps she was simply confused.

Still, in the back of her mind, Winifred detected the nagging realisation that although she cared for Lord Haverton, she did not wish to kiss him. In fact, her heart steered her in another direction, and she could not keep herself from remembering the way Trent had kissed her a mere two days ago.

What she had felt then was still indescribable to her, and for that very reason it had terrified her more than anything else she had ever experienced. How could she feel something she did not understand? After all, there was not a single, logical reason why he should be able to make her feel thus? Constantly, he aggravated her, called her names…

Fred.

A shiver went down Winifred's spine at the memory of his nickname for her on his lips.

"Are you cold?" Lord Haverton asked, his green eyes full of concern.

Shaking off the memory that had claimed her, Winifred forced a reassuring smile onto her face. "Not at all. I was merely…lost in thought."

He chuckled, "It happens to me, too, at times. My father always called me a dreamer." A wistful smile tugged on his lips. "But he was like that himself."

"Has he passed on?" Winifred asked, seeing the sorrow that still rested in Lord Haverton's gaze.

He nodded. "Not two years ago." He swallowed. "I have very fond memories of him. However, I am sad to say that my parents never shared the kind of union that would inspire affection." Inhaling deeply, he remained quiet for a long moment, his gaze holding hers, before he seemed to have come to a conclusion.

Stepping forward, he swallowed, the trace of a nervous smile on his face. "Title notwithstanding, I'm a simple man with simple hopes for the future. I wish for nothing more but a loving wife and a happy family."

Staring at Lord Haverton, Winifred drew in a shaky breath, knowing full well what he was about to say…to ask. She also knew that there was no sensible reason to refuse him.

"My dearest Lady Winifred," Lord Haverton began, tentatively reaching for her hand, "allow me to say that in the short time we've known each other, I've come to admire you greatly."

Winifred swallowed, unable to dislodge the lump in her throat, as panic began to rise in her heart. In a moment, he would ask her to marry him, and she would need to give him an answer. But which one? Was she to accept or refuse?

What was she to do?

"I've thought this through quite thoroughly," Lord Haverton continued, "and I've concluded that—"

"Excuse the interruption," came Griffin's voice from the shadow of the doorway. "However, I'm afraid I must." Stepping into the room, his eyes sought hers, and Winifred could not deny that her heart rejoiced at the reprieve he granted her.

Releasing her hand, Lord Haverton took a step back. "Amberly, I assure you my intentions toward your sister are completely honourable."

Griffin nodded his head in acknowledgement. "Of that I'm certain, Haverton. However, I need to speak to my sister on a matter of urgency. Would you excuse us for a moment?"

"Certainly." Lord Haverton nodded eagerly and left without a moment's hesitation.

Once she was alone with her brother, Winifred felt the air rush from her lungs, and for a short moment, she closed her eyes, her thoughts a chaotic mess.

"Come with me," Griffin said, holding out his hand to her, before he glanced behind her at the tall windows opening the conservatory and those in it to the prying eyes of other attending guests.

With her hand firmly tucked into the crook of her brother's arm, Winifred found herself walking down a long corridor before Griffin opened a large door and ushered her inside. Judging from the rows upon rows of ceiling-high shelves filled with countless books, they had retreated into the library.

"Are you all right?" Griffin asked as his gaze swept over her. "You seem flustered, to say the least."

Swallowing, Winifred nodded. "I'm quite all right." Whatever did that mean? She wondered, realising that her problem had merely been postponed but not solved. At some point, Lord Haverton would

ask for her hand, and then she would have to give him an answer.

Winifred knew that he was exactly the kind of man she ought to marry, and yet…

Turning to her brother, Winifred found him looking at her with serious eyes, a warning resting in their dark brown depths. "Tonight, will decide your future," he finally said. "I hope you know that. You need to make a choice and ask yourself if you truly wish to marry Lord Haverton."

Staring at her brother, Winifred noticed her mouth opening and closing a few times. "Did you…did you know he was going to propose?"

Griffin scoffed. "A blind man could have seen that coming. That man is smitten with you, and you're not being fair to him."

Again, Winifred opened her mouth, only this time to protest her brother's accusation. However, he cut her off with a wave of his hand.

"Be that as it may," he continued, his gaze hard as it held hers, "I'm not the only one who noticed Haverton's intentions. I thought you ought to know that before you make any rash decisions."

This time, Winifred's mouth fell wide open and her eyes bulged. "Trent?" she whispered as another rush of dizziness engulfed her.

Grasping her by the arm, Griffin held her tight, waiting until she stopped swaying. "When we found you and Haverton alone, I had to hold him back." He chuckled, "Otherwise, he would have stormed in, swung you over his shoulder and carried you off like a caveman."

Glaring at her brother, Winifred hissed, "What on earth is so amusing?" In that moment, she could have strangled her brother! What was he thinking making fun of her misery!

"You, my dear Sister," Griffin said without preamble. Then he drew her hands into his and met her eyes, his own suddenly free of all humour. "Listen to me. I know that you're the kind of person who makes a careful plan and then follows it to the smallest detail, afraid that if you venture from your carefully laid-out path, disaster will strike." At this point, he waited, holding her gaze, needing to know if she would contradict him.

However, she did not. After all, he was right. There was no denying that.

"But despite everything you thought you wanted," Griffin continued, "now is the moment when you need to be absolutely certain of what you want…before you make the wrong choice."

With a frown drawing down her brows, Winifred stared up at

her brother, willing herself to ignore the growing panic that took hold in her heart. "But you chose Lord Haverton for me? Why would you now object?"

Shaking his head, Griffin looked at her as one would a foolish child. "I chose a man who suited you according to your wishes, yes. However, as good a man as Haverton is—and believe me, I have no reasonable objections," Winifred groaned at his words, "he is not the man I would have chosen for you on my own."

As bright spots began to dance before her eyes, Winifred tried her best to keep her breathing under control.

"Whether you like it or not, I still believe you need to follow your heart," he told her, his hands gently squeezing hers, "and it does not lie with Lord Haverton, does it?"

Unable not to, Winifred shook her head.

A pleased smile came to her brother's face. "I know that Lord Haverton is a man who suits you. However, I could also point you in the direction of a man who loves you." His gaze held hers. "It's your choice."

In that moment a shadow fell over her, and Winifred turned her head to see Trent standing in the doorway. "Can I speak to you?" he asked as Griffin was already stepping back.

In that moment, Winifred knew she was lost.

13

FAR FROM SENSIBLE

Trent's hands still shook as he approached, and he remembered only too well the shock that had almost knocked him off his feet when he and Griffin had come upon Winifred and Haverton in the conservatory...alone. Trent had been on the verge of tearing into the room and wreaking havoc when Griffin had grabbed him by the shoulders and told him to leave.

To trust him.

As hard as it had been, Trent had left.

Stepping away from his sister and toward the doorway where Trent stood waiting, Griffin nodded to him. "This is it," he said quietly, glancing at Winifred. "Don't make a mess of things...or I swear you'll regret it." He sighed, "As will I." Then he walked away, leaving them alone.

Shifting his eyes to the woman he loved, Trent inhaled a deep breath.

Something had changed.

Usually, Winifred stood tall, her eyes ablaze, her shoulders thrown back in defiance of anyone who would dare interfere with her plans. Her sharp tongue never failed to hit its mark, and yet, a touch of vulnerability rested underneath her brave exterior, softening her appearance and giving her features the look of kindness and compassion.

Now, all Trent saw was a woman lost.

A woman who did not dare meet his gaze.

And his insides turned to ice. Was he too late? Had Haverton asked for her hand? Had she accepted? Was he speaking to a betrothed woman?

The look of confusion on her face laced with guilt suggested that his hopes had been dashed for good. Still, he had to know. He had to be certain.

As Trent took a step toward her, Winifred's gaze fluttered to meet his for the barest of seconds before it dropped to her trembling hands once more. Then she swallowed, and her feet began to carry her backwards before she turned and approached the tall window, her shoulders relaxing a fraction as her eyes found something safe to gaze upon. "What are you doing here?" Her usually strong voice sounded distant as though far away.

Indeed, what was he doing here?

The truth! A sharp voice hissed, and Trent swallowed, knowing that he would have to risk having his heart trampled if he was to have a chance to secure her hand in marriage. Still, he could not help but remember the moment after he had kissed her two days ago when she had turned panicked eyes on him, sending him away. In her gaze, he had seen that she had been very much aware of his intentions, and still, she had sent him away. It had been clear that she had not wanted him to propose. That had been a mere two days ago. Had anything changed since then? Or would he find himself rejected yet again?

Swallowing, he approached her, stopping at a careful distance, not wishing to frighten her. "I came to ask for your hand in marriage," he said without preamble, his heart hammering in his chest as though he were running a marathon.

At his words, Winifred drew in a sharp breath and a slight shiver gripped her shoulders. Still, she remained quiet, her gaze fixed out the window at the starry night. Agonising moments ticked by before her soft voice reached his ears. "I thought about kissing Lord Haverton tonight."

The shock of her words almost sent him tumbling backwards

and his heart ached as though she had stabbed a knife into it. As though determined to protect him from what was surely to come, his feet carried him closer to the door and the only way out.

But then she suddenly turned around, and his feet immediately rooted him to the spot. Her gaze found his, and for a moment, he thought to see something there he had not expected. Intrigued, he took a step closer. "You did?" he asked, hoping against hope that he had misunderstood her.

Still, she nodded. "I did, but it made me realise," she inhaled deeply, and he could have slapped her for drawing this out, "that I did not wish to."

Trent's heart skipped a beat. "You did not wish to…what?"

The ghost of a smile tickled the corners of her lips, and her gaze dropped from his as though she were embarrassed. "I did not wish to kiss him."

Instantly, unadulterated hope claimed his heart, and for a moment, Trent felt strangely light-headed before the need to see his hope made real claimed him. Stepping toward her, he found her gaze. "The other day when I kissed you," he began, delighting at the soft flush that came to her cheeks, "you kissed me back."

She nodded.

"Why?"

Her gaze narrowed, and her chin rose by a fraction. "I could ask you the same thing," she remarked, her voice steady once more with a touch of annoyance to it.

Trent rejoiced, and a large smile spread over his face.

Obviously annoyed with the absence of a reply, she crossed her arms before her chest, her gaze questioning as it held his. "Why on earth would you wish to marry me?"

Trent laughed, and her eyes narrowed even farther. "Because I love you, Fred," he finally said, and having those words out in the open between them felt incredibly liberating. "Can you not see that?"

She drew in a slow breath as though his answer had shocked her, and yet, her lips seemed more than willing to curl up into a smile…if only she would let them. "Why must you call me that?" she snapped instead, unwilling to allow him off the hook just yet. "It is a most distasteful name. Surely, you could find something more suitable."

"I don't care about suitable," Trent replied, slowly walking toward her, taking note of the way her eyes followed him. "It's my name for you. Only mine." The left corner of her mouth twitched, and Trent could not help but think that his answer pleased her. "A name I can be certain will not be used by another. Or has anyone ever called you that?"

Winifred shook her head, and some of the tension seemed to fall from her as she released the tight grip she'd kept on her own arms. Gesturing wildly as though lost, she opened and closed her mouth, trying to find the words to express herself.

"You're adorable," Trent whispered, completely taken with the honest confusion playing over her features.

As expected, her eyes narrowed. "I'm not a pet, you know?"

Trent laughed, "I don't care what you are as long as you're mine."

"If I were to marry you," she asked suddenly, "would you continue to tease me? To call me by that…name?"

Grinning, Trent nodded. "Would you truly want me to stop?" Closing the remaining distance between them, Trent reached for her hands, surprised to find them rather chilled. Wrapping them with his own, he held her gaze. "More than anything I love seeing your eyes light up with fire," he whispered. "I like the way you snap at me." She rolled her eyes at him and tried to pull her hands out of his grasp, but he would not let her. "It is open and honest and unrestrained. Don't ever stop." Trent chuckled seeing her frowning expression. "It makes you look alive."

Shaking her head, she stared at him. "You cannot be serious. Would you truly wish for a future where you wife snaps at you all the time?"

"If that wife is you," he grinned, "then, yes." Pulling her into his arms, he held her gaze. "Now, tell me, *Fred*," again, she rolled her eyes, "will you marry me? Or do you truly wish to spend the rest of your days with a man who suits you?"

Her eyes narrowed, but the corners of her mouth twitched teasingly. "At least, he would not tease me."

"I do not doubt it."

"He would not snap at me."

Trent grinned. "Very unlikely."

"He would not cover me in paint."

"Never."

A soft smile began to play on her features as all humour left her face. "He would not call me Fred."

"Not if he values his life," Trent growled, his arms tightening around her.

Holding his gaze, Winifred inhaled deeply. "He would not love me the way you do."

Lowering his head to hers, Trent looked deep into her eyes. "Then what is your answer?"

For a long moment she gazed up at him, and Trent tried his best to remain calm, knowing that decisions did not come easy to her. "I'll be your wife," she finally agreed, but held up a warning finger, "however, I shall warn you that the consequences will be dire should you make me regret my decision. Do be certain you want to risk that."

"I *am* certain," Trent whispered as his gaze dropped to her full lips. "As certain as I've ever been." Then he pulled her closer and dipped his head to kiss her.

However, her hands on his chest stopped him.

Frowning, he met her gaze, praying that he had not misunderstood her. "Is something wrong?"

A teasing twinkle in her eyes, she looked at him rather innocently. "I merely thought you wished to know that I love you as well." The corners of her mouth curled up into a wicked grin. "Although I cannot understand why. After all, it is far from sensible."

"Exactly," Trent exclaimed, then drew her into a passionate kiss before she could stop him once more.

EPILOGUE

A few weeks later

inifred had to admit that being married had its perks. Not only was she now free to spend as much time alone with Trent as she wanted, but he had every right to claim her waltzes. Each and every one of them.

And although *Fred* was far from a flattering name, Winifred had come to realise that deep down she had never truly objected to it. It had been more of an obligation, a duty to refuse to be called by such a name. However, in truth, she had always delighted in the knowledge that she was the one and only Trent had thought up a nickname for.

The one and only he had ever loved.

"What do you have against Chad?" she asked as they twirled around the dance floor to yet another waltz. "I cannot call you Wick. That sounds ridiculous."

Now, it was Trent who rolled his eyes. "I don't see why you need to come up with a nickname for me anyways. Trent is already quite short. It's only one syllable whereas Winifred has three."

Winifred snorted, "Don't tell me you only came up with that

unflattering nickname because it was too time-consuming to call me by my given name!"

He grinned. "Fine, perhaps it wasn't the only reason. Still, that doesn't mean you have the right to—"

"That's precisely what it means!" Winifred interrupted, delighting in the way his eyes rolled in annoyance. "After all, I'm your wife, and you are mine to call as I wish."

A large smile spread over his face. "Is that so?"

Winifred laughed at the mischievous twinkle in his eyes, reminding herself how fortunate she was to be married to a man she truly loved. Although she had once thought differently, the past few weeks had proved to Winifred that the two of them were more suited to one another than she had initially thought. Certainly, they still bickered and snapped at one another, called each other names and outright delighted in teasing the other when it was least expected.

Still, Winifred had come to realise that Trent knew her as only her brother did. With one look, he could tell when she was saddened or upset or out of sorts. Although he had no affinity for art, he never tired of discussing her own paintings, offering his opinions and urging her to try something new. He loved to dance, and they spent many nights at home after supper, dancing from room to room. At first, their servants had seemed mildly startled. However, by now, they had accepted their master and mistress's quirks and indulged them with a kind smile.

Life was good. Better than Winifred had ever hoped it would be.

And she had no doubt her mother would have been happy for her. They might have gone down different paths, but was happiness not something everyone hoped for?

When the music came to an end, Trent escorted her to a small group of friends and acquaintances standing off to the side, her brother among them.

A young man with bushy eyebrows inclined his head to them. He was an old friend of Griffin's, only just returned from the continent; however, Winifred could not quite recall his name. "My congratulations on your wedding. From what Amberly told me, he is quite relieved to have his sister well married." He grinned at her brother, a mischievous twinkle in his eyes that reminded her of her husband. "I cannot understand why you had trouble marrying her off. A beauty like her."

Smiling, Winifred felt the muscles in Trent's arm tense as he forced a good-natured grin on his face. "He's a sweet man," she

89

whispered teasingly.

Looking down at her, he rolled his eyes. "You'll be the death of me, woman."

"Only living up to my word," Winifred chuckled, wondering if they would ever tire of these little games. She could only hope that that would never happen.

"Mind you, she had no lack of suitors," Griffin indulged his friend, casting her a wicked grin. "However, I'm afraid my sister was quite particular about the kind of husband she had in mind. I tell you it caused me many sleepless nights."

Everyone laughed at Griffin's played exhaustion, patting him on the shoulder.

Meeting her brother's gaze, Winifred could not keep the words from tumbling out of her mouth. "I suppose that it is now my turn to find my brother a suitable bride."

Roaring laughter echoed around them. Only Griffin suddenly looked at bit ill at ease.

"You're at her mercy now, Amberly!" the man with the bushy eyebrows announced with delight. Then his smiling blue eyes turned to her. "My lady, if you require any assistance, do not hesitate to call on me. I'm quite familiar with a number of eligible ladies and could point you in the right direction."

"How kind of you, my lord." Smiling, Winifred glanced at her brother, who seemed a bit pale suddenly.

"In fact, there are many eligible ladies here tonight," Griffin's old friend continued, unable to drop the subject despite her brother's threatening glares. "However, I would advise against Miss Abbott." He leaned closer into the group and whispered, "She's rumoured to be the most awful woman in all of England."

Intrigued, Winifred nodded, seeing with delight the way her brother's eyes fell open as he realised the danger that lurked in his future. "Oh, no, you wouldn't," he stammered, shaking his head as though that would be able to dissuade her.

Winifred grinned, glimpsing a similarly entertained look on her husband's face. "You gave me your word, dear brother, and besides what's fair is fair." Then she turned to the man with the bushy eyebrows who had followed their exchange with rapt attention. "Would you be so kind as to point out Miss Abbott to me?"

A wide grin spread over his face. "I most certainly would," he replied, winking at Griffin, who groaned in agony.

This season would no doubt prove to be quite entertaining.

Perhaps not for her brother.

Still, one could not hope to please everyone, could one?

ABOUT BREE

USA Today bestselling author, Bree Wolf has always been a language enthusiast (though not a grammarian!) and is rarely found without a book in her hand or her fingers glued to a keyboard. Trying to find her way, she has taught English as a second language, traveled abroad and worked at a translation agency as well as a law firm in Ireland. She also spent loooong years obtaining a BA in English and Education and an MA in Specialized Translation while wishing she could simply be a writer. Although there is nothing simple about being a writer, her dreams have finally come true.

"A big thanks to my fairy godmother!"

Currently, Bree has found her new home in the historical romance genre, writing Regency novels and novellas. Enjoying the mix of fact and fiction, she occasionally feels like a puppet master (or mistress? Although that sounds weird!), forcing her characters into ever-new situations that will put their strength, their beliefs, their love to the test, hoping that in the end they will triumph and get the happily-ever-after we are all looking for.

If you're an avid reader, sign up for Bree's newsletter at www.breewolf.com as she has the tendency to simply give books away. Find out about freebies, giveaways as well as occasional advance reader copies and read before the book is even on the shelves!

Thank you very much for reading!

Bree

CONQUERING HER HEART

#8 A FORBIDDEN LOVE NOVELLA SERIES

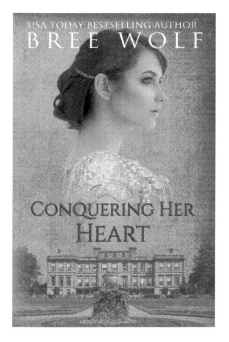

**The most awful woman in England.
An honour-bound gentleman.
And a pact that will benefit them both.**

When ABIGAIL finds herself swarmed with eligible suitors, her only solution to evade a marriage of convenience is to reinvent herself in a most awful way.

Agreeing to his sister's suggestion of choosing each other's spouse, GRIFFIN RAMEY, EARL OF AMBERLY, finds himself confronted with the most awful woman in all of England.

Is there any chance for a happily-ever-after when both parties dislike one another?

Coming July 31, 2018

A FORBIDDEN LOVE
NOVELLA SERIES

For more information, visit

www.breewolf.com

LOVE'S SECOND CHANCE SERIES

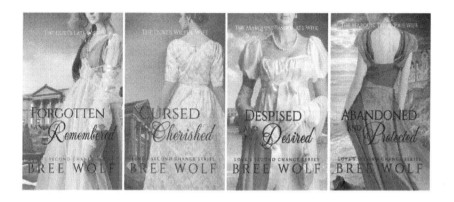

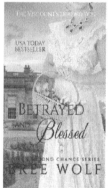
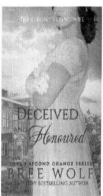

For more information, visit

www.breewolf.com

Made in the USA
Monee, IL
10 December 2019